THE LION
Storyteller
BOOK OF
ANIMAL
TALES

For Noah   B.H.

With love for Bori, and in memory of my parents   K.K.N.

Text copyright © 2002 and 2011 Bob Hartman
Illustrations copyright © 2011 Krisztina Kállai Nagy
This edition copyright © 2011 Lion Hudson

The moral rights of the author and illustrator
have been asserted

A Lion Children's Book
an imprint of
Lion Hudson plc
Wilkinson House, Jordan Hill Road,
Oxford OX2 8DR, England
www.lionhudson.com
ISBN 978 0 7459 6131 6

First edition 2002
This revised and reillustrated edition 2011
10 9 8 7 6 5 4 3 2 1 0

A catalogue record for this book is available
from the British Library

Typeset in 13/16 Century Schoolbook BT
Printed in China May 2011 (manufacturer LH06)

Distributed by:
UK: Marston Book Services Ltd, PO Box 269, Abingdon, Oxon OX14 4YN
USA: Trafalgar Square Publishing, 814 N Franklin Street, Chicago, IL 60610
USA Christian Market: Kregel Publications, PO Box 2607, Grand Rapids, MI 49501

THE LION Storyteller BOOK OF ANIMAL TALES

Retold by Bob Hartman
Illustrations by Krisztina Kállai Nagy

LION
CHILDREN'S

Contents

Introduction

For several years now, both teachers and parents have been asking me to write a collection of animal stories. But until I started reading traditional tales and choosing the ones I wanted to retell I never realized *why* animal stories are so popular. And it's simple. Animal stories are really just stories about us!

Aesop knew that, thousands of years ago. His busy ants, lazy grasshoppers and conceited crows were just a way of exploring some very basic human flaws and virtues. Sometimes those traits were linked to the animals themselves (ants always look pretty busy to me!) but sometimes there was no obvious connection at all (peacocks seem proud, but crows?). Apparent connection or not, attributing human characteristics to particular animals is found in storytelling traditions all over the world. Clever foxes, greedy pigs and nasty wolves people some of the world's most famous legends and tales. And "people" is exactly the right word – because what people do is ultimately what these tales are about.

Because of the breadth of this tradition, I have tried to include stories from every "corner" of the globe. Just for fun, I have also written a few of my own. And I have consciously chosen those stories that I believe encourage the very best human traits. I don't mean to be "preachy", and I don't think the stories have turned out that way. But I do think that stories can encourage children to be more kind or gentle or compassionate – and that's one of my hopes for this book.

Finally, a note about "trickster" tales. Some people may question the value of such stories and worry that they promote deceitfulness. But I would rather focus on the origin of those tales. Stories about rabbits tricking foxes usually come from cultures where one group has dominated or exploited another. The smaller creature becomes a figure of hope – using what it has (usually only its quick wits) to overcome a more powerful adversary. Understood in this context, these stories are about much more than brain over brawn. They are about dignity and resourcefulness. And better still – they are lots of fun!

Maybe that's the most important thing of all. That you and the children in your life should have fun with these stories. Fun at home. Fun in class. Fun at bedtime. And that the fun and the stories will help you better understand who you are and bring you closer together.

Bob Hartman

The Fox and the Crow

Fox crept slowly – crept up on Crow.

But as he sprang into the air – red fur flying and white teeth flashing – Crow flew away into the branches of a tall tree.

It was not Crow that Fox wanted, but the fat piece of cheese she held in her beak. So he stood thinking for a moment, and, when he had come up with another plan, Fox trotted towards the tree and called to Crow in his most pleasant voice, "Crow! Dear Crow, I'm sorry I startled you. I was just overcome, that's all."

Overcome? wondered Crow silently. And she stared at Fox, confused.

"How else can I put it?" Fox said. "It is rare that one stumbles upon such beauty as yours in this rough and ordinary world."

Crow stared, more puzzled than ever. Beauty? Me? she wondered. And she went to fly away.

"I can tell by your expression," Fox continued, "that you are not following my meaning. Stay with me, just a moment, and I will explain.

"I have seen crows before. Many crows, in fact. But none with such shiny feathers as yours. None with such shapely wings. And certainly none with such deep black eyes."

Crow could not hide her pleasure! This was all a surprise to her. But a wonderful surprise, to be sure. She wanted to say, "Go on. More please!" But there was the cheese to consider and, besides, Fox showed no signs of stopping!

"It is not only your appearance that has touched me," he went on, "but your considerable talent as well. Most birds of your kind would have launched themselves clumsily from the ground. But you soared! The graceful arc of your wings was a picture – no, a poem! – against the evening sky!"

Crow was trembling now, overwhelmed by Fox's flattery. And so she was totally unprepared for what came next.

"Dare I say it?" Fox whispered. "Is it too much to hope for? But is it possible, just possible, that flying is not your only gift? Is it possible that you can also... sing?

"If so, then I would love nothing more than to hear you. Could you...? Would you... (Dare I even suggest such a thing?) ... honour me with just one note from that lovely crow throat?"

Crow could no longer think. She was so taken in by Fox's sweet words that she forgot even the simplest thing – that crows cannot sing. Not even one note.

So Crow opened her mouth, and two things happened.

The most awful "squawk" came out of her beak. And the cheese came out as well!

In fact, it dropped straight to the ground, where Fox gobbled it down in one bite.

"Thank you very kindly," he grinned. "I knew something wonderful would come out of that mouth of yours."

Then he trotted off into the forest, leaving Crow feeling foolish and flattered all at the same time.

9

City Mouse
and Country Mouse

City Mouse went to visit Country Mouse.

He shut the door of his flat. He climbed into the lift. He walked into the garage, hopped into his car and nosed his way out onto the city streets.

He stopped at one light after another, crawling slowly past office blocks and theatres and restaurants.

He sped up a little when he reached the suburbs. He motored past schools and parks and shopping malls, and row after row of houses.

Finally, City Mouse reached the country. Fields flew by, dotted with hungry sheep. Then barns and hedgerows and trees and hills. He drove faster and faster, slowing down only to race around the occasional tractor. And then he stopped. For there, at the side of the road, sat Country Mouse's cosy country cottage.

Flowers filled the front garden, and the back garden too. And there were apple trees and pear trees, and birds singing all around.

The two friends sat in the garden and chatted. They sipped home-made cider and shared simple country meals – bread and cheese and pickle.

But after a few days of this, City Mouse found that he was just a little bit bored.

"This is all very pretty," he said to his friend. "But it's nothing compared to the city! There's so much to see there! So much to do! So much excitement and adventure!"

"Well, let's go then!" squeaked Country Mouse. "Let's go at once!"

So they packed their things, watered the plants and hopped into the car.

And City Mouse took Country Mouse back with him to the city.

They drove fast at first, slowing down only to race around the occasional tractor. They flew past hills and trees and hedgerows and barns, and fields dotted with hungry sheep.

They slowed down when they reached the suburbs, driving past row after row of houses. They motored past shopping malls, parks and schools. And at last they reached the city.

They were barely crawling along now – past restaurants and theatres and office blocks – stopping at one light after another.

Country Mouse pressed his long nose against the window and just stared.

"You were right!" he said, gazing up at the tall, tall buildings. "There is so much to see! So much to do! Let's start at once!"

So they parked the car in the garage and walked out onto the city streets. They tried on fancy clothes, looked at expensive jewellery and ate their dinner at a restaurant so fine that Country Mouse could not even pronounce the names of the food on the menu! But as they walked home, talking and laughing about what they had done, they were suddenly met by a gang of very big and very hungry City Cats.

"What do we do now?" asked Country Mouse.

"We run!" squeaked City Mouse. "I told you the city was exciting!"

And that's what they did, scampering this way and that, through city streets and city alleys, until they had left the City Cats far behind.

They leaned against a city building and huffed and puffed, but before they could catch their breath, they were surprised by a pack of noisy City Dogs!

"What now?" trembled Country Mouse.

"We run again!" squeaked City Mouse. "I told you the city was full of adventure!"

Over city pavements and under city cars they raced until they ducked at last into a hole in a city wall. And while the dogs barked outside, they crept along a narrow, dark passage towards a pinprick of light at the other end.

"I smell cheese!" squeaked Country Mouse.

"Careful!" warned City Mouse, but before he could stop him, his friend was racing to the light at the end of the hole. There was cheese, he could smell it. There was cheese, he could taste it. There was cheese! Lying there, just waiting for him, on top of a contraption made of metal and wood. But just before he could grab it, City Mouse raced to his side and pushed Country Mouse out of the way. And the metal sprang up from the wood and chopped the cheese in half!

"City cheese board?" asked Country Mouse.

"City mousetrap," answered his friend. "I think it's time we went home." So the two friends crept carefully back to City Mouse's flat.

City Mouse slept soundly that night. But Country Mouse tossed and turned. At first, the noise of the traffic kept him awake, but when, at last, he fell asleep, his dreams were filled with cats' teeth and dog growls and the "snap" of waiting traps.

When morning came, City Mouse crawled out of bed and found his friend packing his bags.

"I'm going home," said Country Mouse. "The city may be exciting. It may be filled with adventure. But it's also very dangerous! And I think I would be happier in the country, where I belong."

City Mouse was sad to see his friend go, but he understood, he really did. For he was much happier where he belonged as well.

So the two friends locked up the flat and climbed in the lift and went down to the garage. They hopped into the car. And, crawling through the city, motoring through the suburbs and flying through the country, City Mouse took his friend back home.

Why the Cat Falls on Her Feet

Manabozho walked silently on two feet through the forest. He spied Eagle soaring, two wings wide above the tree tops. He caught Spider skittering, eight feet dancing through the fallen leaves. But he did not hear his enemy, Snake, slithering on no feet behind him more silently still.

"Manabozho thinks he is strong," Snake hissed to himself, "because he walks tall on his two feet. But when he tires, and when he lies down – level with me, on no feet at all – then we shall see who is the strongest!"

Manabozho walked all day. But when, at last, the sun wandered beneath the reach of Eagle's wings, and then beneath the tree tops too, Manabozho leaned his spear against the trunk of an oak and lay down upon the ground.

He said goodnight to Ant, six legs struggling to carry a tiny seed. He winked at waking Possum, hanging one-tail from a nearby branch. But when Manabozho closed his eyes, Snake slipped silently to his side.

Snake reared back his head. Snake opened his mouth. Snake showed his sharp and poisonous fangs. But just as Snake was ready to strike, someone struck him from behind.

It was Cat, who had been hiding in the branches of the tall oak. Cat, who had seen what Snake was about to do and leaped, four feet flying, to stop him.

Cat landed on Snake's back and dug four sets of claws into his shiny skin. He turned to bite her, but she was too quick. Again and again she leaped, claws flashing, screeching and scratching until Manabozho was awakened by her cries. He jumped to his feet, and reached for his spear. But by then, the battle was over. Snake was dead, and Cat stood trembling on her four feet beside him.

"Such bravery must be rewarded!" Manabozho declared. "With your four feet, you have saved my life, and so from this time on, wherever you fall, you will always land on your feet – and those four feet will save *you* as well!"

Big Jack, Little Jack and the Donkey

Big Jack and Little Jack were going to the market. They were going to sell their donkey.

They wanted him to look healthy.

They wanted him to look fit.

They wanted him to fetch the very best price.

So they tied his legs together, slipped a pole between them, hoisted the pole up onto their shoulders and set off for the market.

Along the way, they passed an old woman.

"That is the silliest thing I ever saw!" she said.

"Carrying a donkey to the market!
Surely the donkey should be
carrying you!"

Big Jack looked at Little Jack.

Little Jack looked back.

It seemed a sensible suggestion.

So they untied the donkey. Little Jack climbed onto the donkey's back. Big Jack walked behind. And they set off again for the market.

But, along the way, they passed an old man.

"That is the silliest thing I ever saw!" he said. "A strong, young lad rides on a donkey, while his poor old father has to walk behind. Surely the boy should walk!"

Big Jack looked at Little Jack.

Little Jack looked back.

It seemed a sensible suggestion.
So Little Jack jumped off the donkey's back.
And Big Jack jumped on. And they set off again for the market.

But, along the way, they passed a girl.

"That is the silliest thing I ever saw!" she said. "A father rides while his poor son walks. Surely the boy should ride as well!"

Big Jack looked at Little Jack.

Little Jack looked back.

It seemed a sensible suggestion. So Little Jack climbed onto the donkey –

17

climbed on behind
Big Jack. And they set
off again for the market.

But, along the way,
they passed a boy.

"That is the silliest
thing I ever saw!" he said.
"One poor little donkey with
two people on his back. Surely you should
give that donkey a rest!"

Big Jack looked at Little Jack.

Little Jack looked back.

It seemed a sensible
suggestion. So they both climbed
down off the donkey, and set off
again for the market. But, along the
way, they met the mayor.

"That is the silliest thing I ever saw!" he said. "You two fools walk along
while you have a perfectly good donkey to ride! Surely you should put the
beast to good use!"

Big Jack looked at Little Jack.

Little Jack looked back.

They had both heard enough!

"We will show you something even sillier!" said Big Jack. And he found
another pole.

"The silliest thing you ever saw!" said Little Jack. And he tied
the donkey's legs together.

Then they slipped the pole between the donkey's legs and
hoisted the pole up onto their shoulders.

"That is silly!" said the mayor. "The silliest thing of all!"

"No," said Big Jack, shaking his head. "The silliest
thing of all is trying to make everybody happy!"

"That's right," said Little Jack.

"Because it simply doesn't work."

And Big Jack, Little Jack and
their donkey set off again for the
market.

18

The Lion's Advice

Kwasi and Kwaku were friends. But, as sometimes happens with friendships, one was a better friend than the other.

Kwasi and Kwaku would go hunting. Together they would kill an antelope or a wild pig, and then divide the meat. But somehow, Kwasi would always end up with more meat than Kwaku, which made Kwaku's wife very angry.

"But he's my best friend!" Kwaku would explain to his wife. "On another day, he will surely give the bigger share to me."

But that day never came. Whether it was meat from a hunt, fruit from a tree, or even water from the local watering hole, Kwasi would always end up with more. And no matter how hard his wife argued, Kwaku would always defend his greedy friend.

One cool evening, Kwasi and Kwaku went hunting.

"I will say something this time," Kwaku promised himself. "And surely my friend will give me the bigger share."

But as the two friends walked slowly through the bush, there was suddenly no time for thinking. A lion leaped out of the tall grass and decided that two friends would make a much better dinner than one little antelope. Kwasi and Kwaku ran straight for a tree – it was their only chance to escape! Kwasi reached the tree first and shimmied up the trunk to the first branch. But when Kwaku – who was not very good at climbing trees – asked for a hand up, his friend refused to help!

"I'm sorry," said Kwasi. "But there's only room for one on this branch."

"There are other branches!" cried Kwaku.

"Yes," nodded Kwasi. "But you must step on this branch to get to the others. And it could break beneath the two of us – so surely it's better that one of us survives…"

"But I thought you were my friend!" shouted Kwaku, as the lion padded closer.

"I am your friend," Kwasi assured him, "and here's a bit of friendly advice. Someone once told me that a lion will not eat dead meat. So lie down, quietly, with your face to the ground.

And perhaps the lion will think you're dead and find something else for his supper."

Kwaku could not believe this was happening, but the lion was nearly upon him, so he threw himself, face down, to the ground, and hoped for the best.

The lion looked up at Kwasi and growled. Then he crept quietly up to Kwaku and began to sniff. He sniffed at Kwaku's feet and at his legs and at his back and at his shoulders. And finally, he sniffed for what seemed to Kwasi a very long time at Kwaku's head. Then the lion roared and shook his mane and ran away!

When he was certain that the lion would not return, Kwasi leaped down from the tree and pulled Kwaku to his feet.

"That was a lucky break!" he grinned. But Kwaku did not return his smile.

"What's the matter?" asked Kwasi, looking carefully at his friend. "I see no bite marks. As far as I could tell, the lion only sniffed at you."

"No," said Kwaku, shaking his head. "The lion did much more than that. The lion spoke to me."

"Spoke to you?" cried Kwasi, amazed.

"Yes," answered Kwaku solemnly. "The lion told me that my wife was right – I was a fool to think you were my friend. And, in future, I should choose my companions more carefully."

Then he turned and walked sadly away, leaving his companion to wonder if the lion had really spoken, or if Kwaku had finally realized that Kwasi was not truly his friend after all.

21

The Dog and the Wolf

One moonlit night, Wolf went out hunting. Hours passed, and he had nothing to show for all his hard work. He was hungry and he was tired, so he sneaked into Farmer's yard, in the hope of finding a stray duck or chicken. But all he found was Dog!

Dog growled and bared his teeth. But before he could raise the alarm, Wolf crept over to him and whispered, "Brother Dog, keep quiet, I beg you. I have not come to steal. No, I simply wanted to ask about your health. It has been so long since we've talked."

Dog could not remember ever having spoken to Wolf before. But he did seem genuinely interested in having a conversation. And it did get lonely out in the yard at night. So Dog stopped his growling and began, instead, to talk.

"I'm very well, actually," he said. "Thank you for asking." And not wanting to be rude, he asked in return, "How are you?"

Wolf glanced around the farmyard – not a chicken in sight!

"Ah well, I've had better days," he confessed.

"I can see that," Dog admitted. "You look like you haven't eaten for ages! (Dog had a lot to learn about tact!) As for me, well, as you can plainly see, I get plenty to eat. Dog food, twice a day – and scraps from Farmer's table!"

"Really?" said Wolf, suddenly just a little jealous. "I had no idea."

"There's more!" Dog went on (he was enjoying this conversation!). "When I'm tired, I don't have to find some hard spot on the ground to sleep. No, I can curl up in my own little house, here!"

"A house of your own!" nodded Wolf. "Very nice." And he thought about the night before, when he'd tried to sleep, wet and shivering, in the rain.

"And if it gets too cold," Dog continued, "Farmer will often let me sleep inside, right in front of the fireplace!"

"Oooh!" sighed Wolf. "I bet that's cosy!" Now he had forgotten all about chickens and ducks. He just wanted to hear more about Dog. And Dog was happy to oblige.

"Where do I start?" he said. "Playing 'catch' in the fields. Doggie treats at Christmas. And do you see this shiny coat of mine? Farmer's wife combs it and brushes it and pulls out every burr and twig."

Wolf was impressed. So impressed, in fact, that he couldn't help blurting out, "I wish I was a dog!"

"Well, why not?" said Dog. "We need someone to watch the other side of the yard. And you've got what it takes – sharp teeth, a keen sense of smell, plus you know all the prowlers' tricks!"

"Let's go!" cried Wolf. "Let's talk to Farmer now!"

But Dog grew suddenly quiet.

"We'd best wait till morning," he said. "Farmer doesn't like to be wakened. And, besides, there's the small matter of this chain."

Wolf looked closely, and, yes, there was indeed a chain attached, at one

end, to a post in the ground. And fastened, at the other end, to something round Dog's neck.

"And what's that?" asked Wolf, pointing to the collar.

"That?" Dog shrugged. "That's just Farmer's way of saying that he owns me."

"Owns you?" asked Wolf. And as he said it, he started to creep slowly away.

"What's the matter?" asked Dog. "Don't you want to live here any more?"

"No thank you," said Wolf. "A full belly, a warm fireplace and a roof over my head sound very nice indeed. But they are not worth the price of my freedom!"

Then Wolf turned and ran off into the moonlit night – hungry, yes, but free.

The Kind Parrot

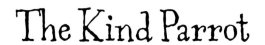

Hunter went into the jungle to hunt. He hunted
for rabbits. He hunted for squirrels. He hunted
for deer and monkeys and wild pigs. But every
time he raised his bow, his prey jumped or ducked or
scurried out of sight.

  Hunter was hungry. Hunter was tired. And then Hunter
saw a parrot, bright yellow and blue, in the branches of a tree.
So Hunter raised his bow. And Hunter aimed straight and true. But as he
went to release the arrow, Hunter heard the parrot squawking a little song:

> *Hunter be good. Hunter be kind.*
> *Spare my life and you will find*
> *A reward, a promise, sure and true.*
> *Goodness and kindness will return to you.*

Hunter dropped the arrow.
Hunter lowered his
bow. And as he did, the
parrot flew away,
bright yellow
and blue, into
the jungle.

And that's when Hunter heard a sound. Something was running through the jungle – running right at him through the bushes and the trees. It could have been a panther, a hyena or a wolf. He could not tell. He could not see. So, afraid, he let an arrow fly. But when he went to see what he had killed, he realized that it was not an animal at all. No, it was the brother of one of the most important men in his village!

Hunter was heartbroken. He carried the man's body back to the village. He tried to explain what had happened. He told the village elders that it was an accident. But no one believed him. And so they sentenced him to die!

On that very day, however, the village was visited by the king. Hunter's wife went to the king. She explained what had happened. She begged him to save Hunter's life.

The king listened carefully to her story. And then he gave her his decision.

"I will give your husband one chance to save himself," the king said. "A test, to see if he is telling the truth. Tonight, we will have a party in the village to celebrate my visit. We will all be dressed in costumes. If your husband can pick me out of the crowd, then his life will be spared."

The woman hardly knew what to say. Her husband had a chance – yes. But how would he ever pick out the king?

26

As soon as the party had begun, the guards were told to bring Hunter to the middle of the village. Just as the king had said, everyone was dressed in costume. Some looked like animals. Some looked like clowns. And Hunter's wife wept when she saw that many were dressed like kings!

She looked at her husband, but Hunter just sighed. Try as he might, he could not spot the king. He lifted his eyes to heaven, to pray for help. And just at that moment, Hunter saw something else – a flash of colour, bright yellow and blue, in the branches above his head. And then he heard a squawking voice that he recognized at once:

> *Hunter be good. Hunter be kind.*
> *You spared my life and now you will find*
> *A king wearing rags, nothing shiny or new.*
> *Goodness and kindness will return to you.*

Hunter peered into the crowd, and, sure enough, there among all the fancy costumes stood someone dressed as a beggar.

"That's him!" cried Hunter. "That's the king! The one dressed in rags!"

And as soon as he'd said it, the crowd erupted in laughter.

"Ridiculous!" sniggered one of the guards.

"He's finished!" snorted another.

But when the beggar removed his rags and took off his mask, it was indeed the king.

"Set him free!" the king commanded. "A man wise enough to see a king through a beggar's robes must surely be telling the truth!"

And so Hunter's life was spared. He joined in the party, of course – he had more to celebrate than anyone there. And as he walked home with his wife, he caught sight of the parrot, bright yellow and blue. And heard the bird squawk one last time:

> *Hunter be good. Hunter be kind.*
> *Remember this day and you will find*
> *That you spared my life, I saved yours too!*
> *Goodness and kindness have returned to you.*

The Tortoise and the Hare

Tortoise was slow. Very slow.

He walked slowly. And he talked slowly. And when he ate his dinner, he chewed each bite slowly, a hundred times or more.

Hare, however, was fast. Very fast.

He never walked anywhere. He ran.

He talked so quickly that his friends hardly understood what he said.

And as for his dinner – well, he gobbled it down before anyone else could even start.

Hare liked to laugh at Tortoise.

"Slowcoach." That's what he called him. And "Slow-mo" and "Mr Slowy Slow".

Tortoise put up with this for a long time (he was slow to get angry as well). But one day, Tortoise had had enough. So he turned to Hare and said (very slowly, of course), "Why don't you race me, then?"

Hare fell over in fits of laughter. He giggled and snorted and chuckled and guffawed, all in one quick breath.

"Of course I'll race you!" he answered. "I'll run so fast you won't even see me!"

The day of the race arrived, and Hare's friends gathered round to cheer him on.

"I'll beat him! I'll crush him! I'll run him into the ground!" chattered Hare. And he spoke

so quickly that all his friends could answer was:

"Eh?"

And "Huh?"

And "What did he say?"

But they clapped him on the back and cheered anyway.

There was no one, however, to support Tortoise, because no one wanted to be seen with a loser.

So he waited patiently at the starting line, slowly stretching one leg and then another, hoping to avoid any painful tortoise cramps.

At last, someone shouted, "Ready. Steady. Go!"

Hare leaped from the line and raced off so quickly that he soon disappeared over the first hill. But Tortoise just plodded slowly along – one foot in front of the other – determined to do his best.

Mile after mile flashed by as Hare raced past cars and motorbikes and trains.

And Tortoise plodded on, step by slow step, stopping now and then to give way to the odd, passing snail.

In no time at all, the finishing line was in Hare's sight. A crowd of animals was on the other side, waiting to cheer his victory. But instead of rushing over it, he decided to have one last laugh at Tortoise's expense.

He waved to the crowd, pointed to a shady tree and then settled down for a little nap.

"I'll show them," he chuckled. "I can sleep half the day and still beat that slowcoach!"

So Hare fell asleep, while Tortoise plodded on.

Hare dreamed of Tortoise and his four short plodding legs. He dreamed of his own legs – long and strong and fast. Then he dreamed of the race and the finishing line and the cheering crowds. And then, suddenly, he was dreaming no longer. He was awake! But the crowds were, somehow, still cheering.

Hare opened his eyes and peered at the crowd. They were shouting and raising their hands in the air. But how could that be? He was still under the tree. And that's when Hare saw Tortoise – only inches away from the finishing line! And then Hare looked at the sun. It had almost dipped below the hills, for with all his dreaming he had slept the day away!

Hare leaped to his feet. He raced. He rushed. He fairly flew. But Tortoise just kept plodding. And even though Hare strained every last muscle in his long strong legs, Tortoise managed to plod over the line just a step ahead!

"It's not fair!" chattered Hare. "I was there! By the tree! You all saw me!"

"Eh?" said the crowd.

And "Huh?"

And "What did he say?"

Then everyone rushed to Tortoise and lifted him in the air, cheering and shouting his name. While Hare was left alone, huffing and puffing and complaining away, nursing one painful hare cramp!

Why Dogs Chase Cats and Cats Chase Mice

"Hear ye, hear ye!" said the king. "I have a very important announcement to make. A dog saved my life yesterday, and so, from this moment on, all dogs are to be treated with the utmost respect.

"Food and water dishes must always be full.

"Toys and balls must be bright and bouncy.

"Playing fetch is now our national sport.

"And dog-catchers are officially unemployed!"

Then the king held up a large piece of paper.

"Here is my decree!" he announced. "Signed with my name and sealed with my stamp. I am giving it to the dogs for safe keeping."

"Woof, woof!" barked the dogs, as Dalmatian trotted forward to receive the paper. This was the happiest day of their lives. And they yipped and yapped and wagged their tails in celebration.

But when the day came to an end, the dogs were faced with a problem. Where should they keep that very important piece of paper? The dogs sniffed and scratched, barking out the best ideas they could think of.

"Dig a hole!" suggested Dachshund.

"And bury it!" added Beagle.

"It's not a bone!" sighed Spaniel. "It's a piece of paper. The dirt will ruin it."

"I know," woofed Dalmatian, at last. "Why don't we ask the cats to take care of it? They're clever – they'll know exactly what to do!"

"Excellent idea!" woofed the others in reply, for in those days dogs and cats were great friends.

So the king's decree was given to the cats for safe keeping. And they, too, held a meeting. They stretched and spat and cleaned their claws, miaowing out the best ideas they could think of.

"Climb a tree!" suggested Siamese.

"And hide it there!" added Tabby.

"But it's a piece of paper!" moaned a Manx. "The first gust of strong wind will blow it away!"

"I know!" purred Persian. "Why don't we give it to the mice? They're very good at hiding things."

"Excellent idea!" purred the others in reply, for in those days cats and mice were great friends too.

So the king's decree was given to the mice. And because hiding was, indeed, their speciality, there was no need for a meeting. The mice simply tucked the paper away in a safe, warm mouse hole.

And that would have been the end of the story, if one little mouse had not got a bad case of the nibbles.

He could have nibbled on a bit of carpet. He could have nibbled on a bit of wood. He could have nibbled on a nice bit of cheese. But this little mouse chose, instead, to nibble on

a nice bit of paper.
And, sadly, the paper
he nibbled on was the
king's own decree.

He only nibbled a little
at first. But once he'd started
nibbling, he just had to go on and on. And the nibbling
didn't stop until the paper had been nibbled clean away.

Unfortunately, it was at that very moment that a
particularly nasty dog-catcher found his way into the
kingdom. He picked up his net and climbed out of his
wagon and set to work.

But the first dog he caught howled in protest.

"You can't do this to me! The king himself has
forbidden it."

"Really?" growled the dog-catcher. "Then prove it!"

So the dogs went to the cats, and the cats went to the mice.
And when the mice went to the mouse hole, all they found was
one fat little mouse with the odd bit of paper clinging to his
nibbling teeth.

"Yow!" cried the cats, when the mice told them the sad
news.

"A-woo!" howled the dogs, when they talked to the cats.

And no one was great friends with anyone any more.

So the cats chased the mice.

And the dogs chased the cats.

And the dog-catchers chased the dogs.

And, sadly, it has been that way ever since.

Rabbit and the Briar Patch

Things always seemed to go right for Rabbit. Perhaps that's because he was so clever. Or perhaps it was because he had more than his fair share of lucky rabbit's feet!

One day, however, things didn't go so well. He was just whistling his way through the fields when Fox leaped out from behind a tree and grabbed him by the throat!

"Got you now!" Fox snarled. "And there's no escape!"

Rabbit struggled and Rabbit squirmed.

Rabbit fidgeted and Rabbit fought.

And just as he was about to give up hope, Rabbit noticed a briar patch down at the end of the field.

"I suppose you're right," Rabbit sighed. "It's all over for me now. I will surely end up in your stewpot. But at least it's better than getting chucked into that old briar patch."

"Stewpot?" asked Fox. "I don't have a stewpot! And besides, making stew would just give you time to slip away. No, I intend to barbecue you, Rabbit, right here where we stand!"

"That's fine by me," said Rabbit, tossing a worried look at the edge of the field. "Stick me on a spit. Turn me over the fire. Dip me in your sweetest sauce. But please, oh please, don't chuck me into that briar patch!"

Fox glanced at the briar patch too. He couldn't imagine what was worrying Rabbit. But he had more important plans – dinner plans!

"Barbecuing's too messy!" he decided. "I think I'll make a sandwich out of you instead."

"Oh yes!" exclaimed Rabbit. "That would be wonderful! Shove me between two thick slices of bread. Lay me down on a bed of lettuce and cover me with mayonnaise. But please, oh please, don't chuck me into that briar patch!"

Fox was getting very confused now. And very hungry.

"Even a sandwich is too much trouble!" he snapped. "I believe I'll just gobble you down, right here and now!"

"That would be so thoughtful!" cried Rabbit. "Swallow me down, skin and bone. Crunch me up into a thousand itty bitty, little pieces. But please, oh please, don't chuck me into that briar patch!"

"Then that is exactly what I'll do!" howled Fox, at last. "For nothing seems to terrify you more!"

And he picked up Rabbit by both his ears, swung him around in a huge circle and chucked him right across the field and into the briar patch.

Rabbit landed with a "thud". And then out of the briar patch came the

most horrible sounds
that Fox had ever
heard.

Rabbit screamed and
Rabbit squealed.

Rabbit yelped and
Rabbit yowled.

And then everything
went suddenly silent.

Fox crept through the
field. He crept right up to
the edge of the briar patch.
All he had to do was reach in
and grab hold of his dinner.

And that's when Rabbit stuck
his head out on the far side of the
briar patch.

"I was born in the briar patch!" he
grinned.

"I was raised in the briar patch!" he grinned some more.

"And now I'll say goodbye to the briar patch!" he grinned for the last
time. "And to you too, Fox!" Then he turned and ran away, a happy rabbit
again. Maybe because he had more than his fair share of lucky rabbit's feet!
Or perhaps because he was so clever!

The Crocodile Brother

Once upon a time, there were two tribes who simply could not get along with each other. It started with a stolen cow, then a few missing pigs. Hard words followed, then threats. And when the eldest son of one of the chiefs was found murdered, everyone prepared for war!

The father of the murdered boy was broken-hearted. But in spite of his anger and his grief, the last thing he wanted was for other fathers to lose their sons as well. So he persuaded the elders of both tribes to come together and try to work out some peaceful solution.

At first, the meeting looked certain to fail. It started with suspicious stares and soon turned into ugly shouting.

But just before the meeting fell apart completely, the chief stood and raised his hands in the air and cried, "Crocodile!"

Everyone fell silent, each head turning this way and that, looking for the beast. And this gave the chief a chance to speak.

"There is no crocodile among us," he said softly. "Not yet, at least. But listen to my story, brothers, please. And perhaps you will see what I mean.

37

"Once there lived a crocodile," the chief began, "who spotted a tasty fat chicken by the side of the river. The crocodile grinned. The crocodile opened its mouth wide. The crocodile showed its rows of sharp, white teeth. But just before the crocodile snapped its jaws shut around its prey, the chicken spoke!

" 'My brother,' begged the chicken, 'please spare my life. Find something else for your supper.'

"These words surprised the crocodile. My brother? he wondered. What does the chicken mean by that? And while he wondered, the chicken slipped away.

"The next day, the crocodile spied a sleek, juicy duck. The crocodile grinned. The crocodile opened its mouth wide. The crocodile showed its rows of sharp, white teeth. But just before the crocodile snapped its jaws shut around its prey, the duck spoke!

" 'My brother,' begged the duck, 'please spare my life. Find something else for your supper.'

"Again the crocodile was shocked. Brother? he wondered. When did I become brother to a chicken and a duck? And as he tried to puzzle it out, the duck slipped away.

"The crocodile was confused. And he was getting hungrier by the hour. So he went to see his friend, the lizard. He told him about the chicken, and he told him about the duck. And as he did so, the lizard nodded and smiled.

" 'I understand completely!' answered the lizard. 'For I am your brother too!'

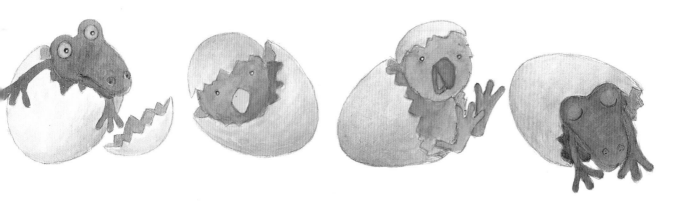

"'My brother?' cried the crocodile. 'How?'

" 'I was hatched from an egg,' replied the lizard. 'And so was the chicken and so was the duck.' And then he smiled at the crocodile. 'And so, my brother, were you! When you think about it, we are more alike than we ever imagined. So why should we want to eat each other?' "

His story finished, the chief turned to the elders.

"My brothers," he said, "we are just like that crocodile."

"Nonsense!" called out one of the elders. "I was never hatched from any egg!" And the elders on both sides laughed.

"No," grinned the chief. "But you have eyes and ears and hands and feet, as we all do. And a son – as many of us have as well. We are more alike than we ever imagined. So why should we devour one another in war, when we can live together in peace like brothers?"

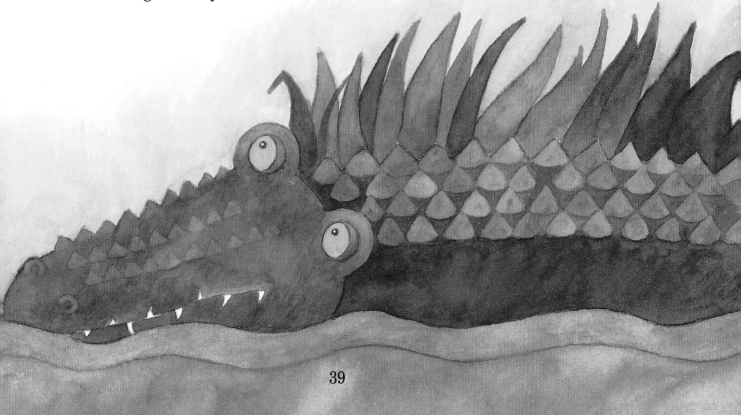

The Boastful Toad

Bull was big. Bull was bulky. Bull was brawny and bulgy and brown.
But despite his size (or, perhaps, because of it!), Bull was no bully.
He was gentle and quiet and bothered no one.

Toad, on the other hand, was tiny. Tinier than Pig,
tiner than Dog, tinier than Cat. And much,
much tinier than Bull.

But despite his size (or,
perhaps, because of it!), he
never stopped saying how
wonderful he was.

"I can jump much
higher than you!" he
boasted to Pig, who
could not jump very
high at all.

"That may be true," Pig
grunted, "but there's no need to point it
out to me."

"I can kill more flies than you!" he
boasted to Dog, who had never eaten an
insect in his life.

"That may be true," woofed Dog, "but
nobody likes a show-off."

"I can swim much further than
you!" he boasted to Cat, who hated
even getting her paws wet.

"That may be true," Cat miaowed,
"but you'd better be careful, Toad. Your
boasting is going to get you into trouble
some day!"

And then, one bright morning, Toad
decided to boast to Bull.

Bull was in his field, chewing on
a thick patch of weeds, when Toad
hopped right up beside him.

40

Toad looked up at Bull, all big and brown and bulky. And he thought hard about his very best boasts.

Bull could jump higher than Toad, there was no doubt about that. Toad had seen him kill hundreds of flies with his tail. And as for swimming, Toad had watched Bull paddle right across the river! So none of those boasts was going to work.

And then he remembered something – a clever trick an old toad had taught him when he was hardly more than a tadpole.

"I can make myself bigger than you!" he shouted at Bull. And Bull nearly choked on his mouthful of weeds.

"That may well be true," said Bull, "but I'm going to have to see it to believe it."

So Toad looked Bull right in the eye. Then he stood up on his tippy toes and sucked in a big breath of air. And sure enough, he blew himself up to twice his size!

"That's an amazing trick," Bull nodded. But it was plain to both of them that Toad was still nowhere near as big as Bull.

"I can get bigger still!" Toad boasted.

41

And he sucked in an even bigger breath of air.

"Now be careful there, little fellow," warned Bull. But Toad was determined to prove that he was right. And he blew himself up to four times his size! But he was still much smaller than Bull. So he started to suck in another big breath of air.

"I think you should stop right there," said Bull.

But Toad kept on sucking in air.

"It's not important how big you are," Bull snorted. "It really isn't!"

But Toad still kept on sucking in air.

"All right. You can make yourself bigger than me. I believe it," said Bull. "Just stop. Please!"

But it was plain to Toad that he was still not big enough. Not yet. So he shut his eyes and concentrated and sucked in one more breath of air…

All the other animals heard a "bang" somewhere off in the fields. And when they went to investigate, Bull was standing there, shaking his big brown head.

"I told him to be careful," Bull sighed. "I warned him."

"I know," miaowed Cat. "I told him that his boasting would get him into trouble one day."

And so it had. For with all his boasting and puffing himself up, poor Toad had blown himself into a million tiny pieces.

The Clever Mouse Deer

The King of All Tigers in the Jungles of Java called for his tiger friends.

"There is not enough meat in the Jungles of Java!" the King of All Tigers roared.

"Not enough elephants.

"Not enough pigs.

"Not enough monkeys and apes."

So the King of All Tigers in the Jungles of Java pulled a whisker from his tiger face.

"Take this to the King of All Beasts in Borneo and tell him that we are coming.

"To eat up his elephants.

"To eat up his pigs.

"To eat up his monkeys and apes."

"And if the King of All Beasts, all the beasts in Borneo, should try and stand in our way, then tell the King of All Beasts in Borneo that we will happily eat him up too!"

So the friends of the King of All Tigers in the Jungles of Java sailed across the sea.

And when they arrived on the shores of Borneo, what did the tigers find?

A Mouse Deer, that's all – a creature both frail and small.

"The King of All Tigers in the Jungles of Java has a message for your king. Give him this whisker. Tell him we're coming – coming to eat up his meat!"

The Mouse Deer ran off into the Jungles of Borneo, wondering what to do.

For there *was* no King of All Beasts in Borneo to give the message to!

The Mouse Deer was frail. The Mouse Deer was small. But the Mouse Deer was clever as well. So she went to her friend, the porcupine, and asked her for one sharp quill.

"You're meat, and I'm meat!" the Mouse Deer explained. "And the tigers will eat us both! But if you give me just one of your quills, I think I can make them go!"

So the Mouse Deer ran back through the Jungles of Borneo with the quill between her teeth.

When she got to the shores of Borneo, the tigers were there on the beach.

"So what's the answer?" roared the tigers of Java. "What was your king's reply?"

"The answer is NO," said the Mouse Deer, shaking as she laid the quill at their feet.

"The King of All Beasts – all the beasts in Borneo – gives you his whisker too. Take it back to your king. Tell him come, if he must. But we'll fight him, that's what we'll do!"

The tigers of Java stared at the quill. They trembled at what they saw. If this was a whisker, then imagine the face to which that whisker belonged!

The whisker was huge, the whisker was pointy, the whisker was sharp and fierce!

The King of All Beasts, all the beasts in Borneo, must be some kind of monster, they guessed.

So the tigers of Java climbed back into their boat and sailed home across the sea.

And when the King of All Tigers saw the whisker, he changed his plans at once!

And that's why, today, in the Jungles of Java, you may still hear a tiger's call.

But among the beasts, the beasts of Borneo, there are no tigers at all!

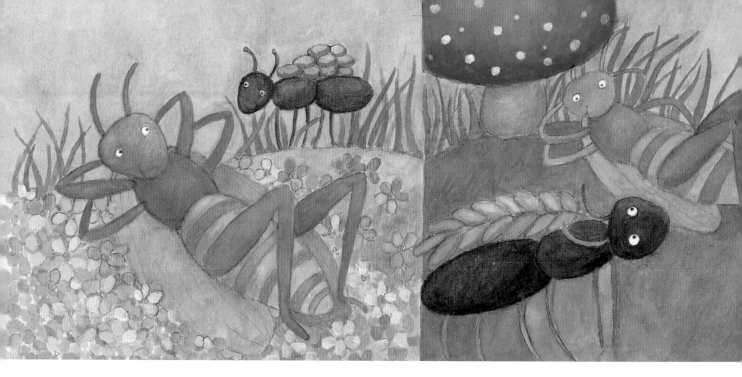

The Ant and the Grasshopper

It was a sunny spring morning.

Grasshopper lay on a bed of apple blossoms, counting the birds in the sky.

Ant hurried past, seeds piled high on his back.

"Come and sit with me for a while!" called Grasshopper. "You work too hard!"

"Can't," said Ant. "Winter is coming, and I need to feed my children."

It was a hot summer afternoon.

Grasshopper lay in the shadow of a toadstool, chewing on a piece of straw.

Ant hurried past, his back bent under a grain of wheat.

"Come and sit with me for a while!" called Grasshopper. "You need the rest."

"Can't," said Ant. "Winter is coming, and I need to feed my children."

It was a crisp autumn evening.

Grasshopper lay on a pile of crunchy leaves, staring up at the stars.

Ant hurried past, struggling with a piece of apple.

"Come and sit with me for a while!" called Grasshopper. "You'll wear yourself out!"

"Can't," said Ant. "Winter is nearly here. I need to feed my children. And perhaps," he added, "perhaps you need to store up some food as well."

"I have plenty of food at the moment," Grasshopper shrugged. "I'll worry about winter when it comes."

It was a bitter winter night.

Grasshopper huddled, hungry, between a stone and the trunk of a bare-branched tree, wishing he had something to eat.

Ant hurried past, straining against the winter wind.

"Come and sit with me for a while!" called Grasshopper. "And perhaps you could spare me something to eat."

"Can't," said Ant sadly. "I wish I could, but I can't. I worked all through the spring and the summer and the autumn, and still have barely enough to feed my children. If only you had worked a little – and thought a little more about the future – then you would have something to eat as well."

Big Jack, Little Jack and the Farmer

Big Jack and Little Jack were going to market.

Along the way, they passed the house of their friend Farmer Fred. So they stopped by to ask if there was anything he needed.

But Farmer Fred wasn't in the house. And he wasn't in the barn. And he wasn't in the farmyard either.

Big Jack and Little Jack were just about to leave, in fact, when they heard whooping and hollering from the hen house.

So they followed the sound, and that's where they found Farmer Fred, jumping up and down for joy, with something bright and shiny in his hand.

"Take a look at this, boys!" he shouted. "Then shake the hand of the luckiest man you ever met. 'Cause my chicken here has just laid me a golden egg!"

Big Jack shook Farmer Fred's hand. And Little Jack did too. Then they just stood and stared at that chicken. And stood and stared even harder at that golden egg.

"Can we fetch you anything from the market?" asked Big Jack at last.

"We're on our way there," added Little Jack.

48

"No thank you, boys," grinned Farmer Fred. "I reckon I'll be doing a different kind of shopping from now on. But I appreciate the offer." And then Farmer Fred got a funny look in his eye and added, "And I'd appreciate it if you'd keep quiet about this chicken of mine too!"

The next week, Big Jack and Little Jack went to market again.
Along the way, they passed the house of their friend Farmer Fred. So they stopped by, just in case he needed something.
But he wasn't in the house. It was filled with painters and decorators.
And he wasn't in the barn. It was crammed full of brand-new cars.
And he wasn't in the farmyard either.
Because there wasn't any farmyard any more – just a great big swimming pool!
So they looked in the hen house.

And there was Farmer Fred, with the very special chicken on his lap.

"I know what you boys want!" he snapped. "You're the only ones who know about my golden eggs. Well, you're not getting any, d'you hear?"

"We don't want your golden eggs," said Big Jack.

"No," added Little Jack. "We just wondered if you wanted anything from the market."

"No, I don't. Leave me alone!" shouted Farmer Fred. "I'm the luckiest man you've ever met. And I've got everything I need right here!"

So Big Jack shrugged his shoulders. And Little Jack did too. Then they left Farmer Fred with his chicken and headed down the road to market.

One week went by. Then two weeks. Then three. And, when Big Jack and Little Jack went to market, they passed Farmer Fred's house without stopping.

But on the fourth week, as they passed by, they heard a sad and sorrowful cry.

They looked in the house. It was beautiful! But Farmer Fred wasn't there.

They looked in the barn. The cars were bright and shiny! But he wasn't there either.

They looked in the swimming pool, where the farmyard had been. Still no sign of Farmer Fred.

So, finally, they looked in the hen house. And there he was, staring at a pile of feathers.

"What's the matter?" asked Big Jack.

"Where's your chicken?" added Little Jack.

And Farmer Fred just sobbed and pointed at the pile of feathers.

"Did a fox do that?" asked Big Jack.

"Or a hawk?" asked Little Jack.

"No," sighed Farmer Fred. "I did it myself. I was the luckiest man in the world. But I got tired of waiting for those golden eggs. There were things I needed to buy. So I thought that if I cut her open, I could get all the eggs at once!"

"But there were no eggs inside, were there?" asked Big Jack.

"No eggs at all?" added Little Jack.

"No," sighed Farmer Fred, "and now there won't be any more eggs, either."

"Well at least you have a nice house," said Big Jack.

"And lots of cars. And a swimming pool!" added Little Jack.

"I suppose so," sighed Farmer Fred. "But I wanted so much more!"

"Can we fetch something for you, then?" asked Big Jack.

"We're on our way to the market," added Little Jack.

"No, I'll be fine," sighed Farmer Fred.

So Big Jack and Little Jack headed for the market. But not before they'd said goodbye to "the luckiest man in the world".

Three Days of the Dragon

Once there was a river that flowed between two tribes –
the Tiana and the Aroman.

When the river flowed fast and full, both tribes drank from it – and lived in peace. But when, one year, the water flowed slow and shallow, and there was not enough to drink, the peace turned quickly to war.

Warriors on both sides died. And so Tiana-Rom, chief of the Tiana tribe, came to his elders with an idea.

"The legends say there is a dragon in the far mountains. A dragon who will help any tribe that is willing to sacrifice the life of a brave young girl."

All eyes stared at him in horror, for every elder knew that the chief's own daughter, Tiana-Mori, was the bravest girl in the tribe.

"Yes," he nodded. "I have spoken to her. And my daughter is willing."

The elders looked at one another. With the dragon's help they would surely win. And so, sadly, they agreed.

Tiana-Mori left the next morning. She walked for three days, and finally she came to the dragon's cave. The dragon lay sleeping – the most beautiful creature Tiana-Mori had ever seen. His scales shimmered green and gold, and on top of his head – like a cockerel's comb – ran a ridge of bright red horns.

The dragon opened one green eye.
"Is there something you want?"
he muttered.

"There is," said the girl. "I am the bravest girl in the Tiana tribe. I am here to sacrifice myself so that you will help us defeat our enemy."

"The bravest girl?" said the dragon. "Climb onto my head, and we'll see about that."

Tiana-Mori walked slowly towards the dragon. She climbed past his sharp teeth, up his long nose, and finally onto his head.

"Now sit between the horns," said the dragon. "And hold on tight!"

And without another word, up the dragon flew – high above the mountains, so swiftly that Tiana-Mori could hardly catch her breath.

At first, Tiana-Mori thought that the dragon meant to drop her. But, as she watched the ground below, she realized that he was doing something else – something even more awful. He was taking her home! They landed just outside the village and, as everyone ran to meet them, Tiana-Mori pleaded with the dragon.

"Eat me now!" she cried. "Spare my father from the sight of the thing you must do!"

"Eat you?" said the dragon. "Wherever did you get that idea?"

"The legends," answered Tiana-Mori.

"The legends?" snorted the dragon. "I don't care about legends. There is more than one way to win the help of a dragon. And you have done so with your bravery. Now tell your people that I will help them."

Tiana-Mori scrambled down from the dragon's head and ran to her father to tell him the whole story. At once, he gathered the elders together to make their war plans.

As a reward for her bravery, Tiana-Mori was invited to the meeting too. Then she went to find the dragon and tell him everything that she had heard.

But the dragon was not interested. He was lying on his back, while the Tiana children bounced on his belly, and their mothers watched and laughed.

"Dragon!" cried Tiana-Mori. "Don't you care about our plans? You and you alone can win the hearts of our warriors and lead them to victory!"

The dragon looked straight into Tiana-Mori's eyes.

"There is more than one way to win the heart of a people," he said. "Listen to the laughter of the children. Then go and ask your warriors if they really want to turn that laughter into tears."

"I don't understand!" shouted Tiana-Mori. "Are you saying you no longer want to defeat our enemy?"

"I have promised. And I will help," the dragon grinned. "If all goes well tomorrow, the Aroman will no longer be your enemy. And perhaps then you will understand." Then, to the cheers of the children below, he flew up into the evening sky.

The next morning dawned drizzling and grey, and the dragon listened patiently to Tiana-Rom.

"Go before us," said the chief. "Terrify our enemy. Then stretch yourself over the river bed and be the bridge we cross to crush them!"

Everything went to plan, at first. The dragon stomped out in front of the Tiana warriors and the Aroman warriors shook with fear. But when the dragon reached the middle of the river, he stopped. He stood between the two tribes. And he spoke: "People of Tiana! People of Aroman! Once you lived in peace. You can live that way again! I have come to show you how."

"Peace?" cried Tiana-Rom. "When we are so close to victory? Never!"

And in his rage, Tiana-Rom let one arrow fly – an arrow that struck the Aroman chief and killed him where he stood.

"See!" he shouted to the dragon. "The legends were right. This is what you have come for – not for peace, but to help us defeat our enemy!"

And so pleased was Tiana-Rom that he did not see the arrow shot in return – the arrow that would surely have pierced his own heart, had someone not leaped in the way.

"Tiana-Mori!" cried the chief in horror. But it was too late. His only daughter lay dying in his arms.

"The legends!" roared the dragon. "The sacrifice of a brave young girl. A dragon's help. Now I will show you what the legends really mean!"

And as the arrows flew thick and fast, and more warriors fell, the dragon tore into the sky. Higher and higher he soared, till he was but a bright speck among the dark clouds. Then he dived straight towards the earth, faster than the driving rain – until he struck the river with a mighty crash!

The force of his landing knocked the warriors from their feet. When they rose and looked, the dragon was gone, but the river was flowing fast and full!

Green and gold the water shimmered. Then a voice called out from the deep. "There is not much time. Come together to the river. Wash your dead in the water and they will live."

So that is what the tribes did. Tiana-Rom went first, carrying Tiana-Mori. And the Aroman followed with their fallen chief. And there, in the river, the warriors of Tiana and the warriors of Aroman came back to life!

But that was not all. As they waded and splashed, the people of Tiana and Aroman looked into each other's faces once again. And they remembered the days when the river was full – the days when they lived in peace. And so it was that their friendship came back to life as well.

They embraced one another, and so caught up were they in their reunion that they did not notice the bridge – a ridge of bright red horns, like a cockerel's comb – that grew from one side of the river to the other.

Later, as the tribes celebrated their peace, Tiana-Mori sat on the bridge and stared into the water.

"I'll miss you," she said. "And I'm sorry that I did not trust you. But I understand now. I really do. There's more than one way to do everything. To win the help of a dragon. To win the heart of a people."

"Yes," rose a voice from the river. "And there's more than one way to win a battle too."

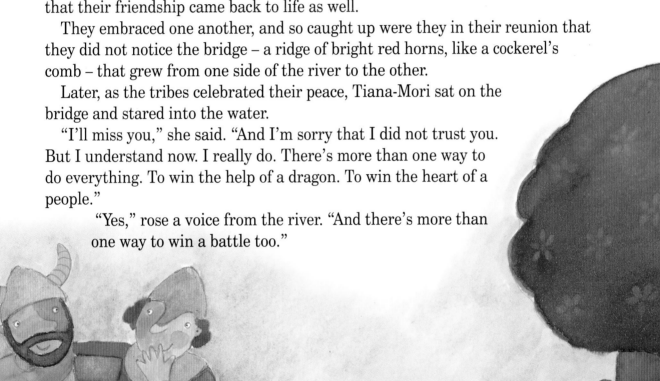

How the Turkey Got Its Spots

In the African bush, there lives a wild turkey, who is covered all over with bright white spots. But it was not always so. For, once upon a time, the wild turkey was as black as night. This is the story of how the turkey got her spots.

One evening, as Turkey scratched her way through the dry and dusty bush, she spotted a young lion, creeping up on her best friend, Cow. Lion looked hungry – very hungry indeed. And Cow had no idea that he was behind her. So Turkey did the cleverest and bravest thing she could think of. She raced between Lion and Cow, wings flapping, tail dragging and kicking up clouds of dry bush dust.

Lion coughed and sneezed and tried to shake the dust from his eyes. Cow heard him and hurried away. And when the dust had settled and Lion could finally see, Cow was gone! There was no trace of her, for the dust had covered even her hoofprints.

All he could find, in fact, were a few black tail-feathers.

"Turkey!" Lion growled. And he vowed to remember what she had done.

The next evening, Turkey scratched her way to the watering hole. And there was Lion again, tail twitching, creeping closer to Cow than he had been the night before!

Once again, Turkey was determined that Lion would not have her friend for his supper. So, once again, she raced between them, wings flapping, tail dragging and kicking up clouds of dust. And, once again, Lion coughed and sneezed – and failed to catch his supper.

"Turkey!" he roared. But both she and Cow were, by then, long gone.

And so, the next evening, it was not Cow that Lion stalked. No, he went hunting for Turkey. And he found her, at last, leading her little family of chicks back to their nest.

"Gotcha!" Lion roared, as he sprang into the air and bared his claws. But Turkey was not only clever; she was also quick. And before Lion could land, she scooted out of his way, screeching and flapping her wings to send her children running for cover.

Then she pecked at Lion, first at his head, then at his shoulders and at his back. He leaped and twisted and clawed the air. And when he was thoroughly confused, she raced off into the bush, leading him away from her fleeing chicks.

As she ran, Turkey passed Cow, who was grazing behind a big bushy tree.

"Come here, my friend!" called Cow. "Come quickly!" And when they were both safely behind the tree, Cow dipped the tip of her tail into her milk and sprinkled it over her friend. Soon Turkey was no longer black, but covered all over with bright white spots!

59

Turkey flapped out from behind the tree, just as Lion raced by. And because she now looked so different, Lion did not know who she was!

"Have you seen Turkey?" he panted. "She's a big bird – about your size – but black all over."

Turkey shook her head. But she did not say a word, for fear that she would give herself away.

So Lion roared off again, leaving Turkey and Cow chuckling to themselves.

"Quick!" said Cow, "Fetch your chicks and I will give them spots as well."

So that's what Turkey did. And ever since, the wild turkey has not only been clever and quick, but, as a sign of her bravery and kindness, she has been covered all over with bright white spots.

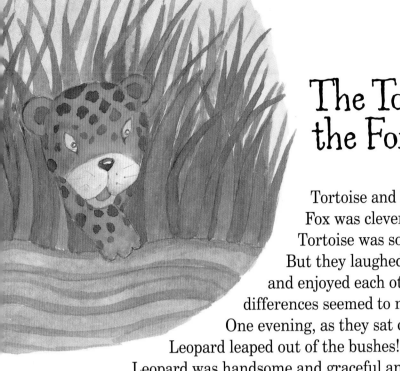

The Tortoise and the Fox

Tortoise and Fox were unlikely friends.
Fox was clever and quick and sleek.
Tortoise was solid and heavy and slow.
But they laughed at each other's jokes
and enjoyed each other's company, and their
differences seemed to make no difference at all.
One evening, as they sat chatting by the riverside,
Leopard leaped out of the bushes!

Leopard was handsome and graceful and dangerous. Fox saw him at once and, because he was clever and quick, darted away from Leopard's sharp claws. But poor Tortoise was not so lucky. Because he was solid and slow, all he could do was pull his head and legs into his lumpy shell and hope for the best. Leopard scooped Tortoise up, scooped him right up out of the riverside mud. He scratched at the shell with his strong sharp claws. Inside, Tortoise shuddered. And outside, hiding safely behind a tree, Fox shuddered as well.

Then Leopard gnawed at the shell, biting down hard with his shiny white teeth. Inside, Tortoise shivered with fear. And outside, his friend Fox shivered too. The shell was lumpy and the shell was hard, but both Fox and Tortoise knew that it wouldn't be long before Leopard gnawed his way inside.

And so Fox – clever, quick Fox – called out to Leopard from behind the tree.

"Leopard, O Leopard!" he barked. "You're doing that all wrong! I'm a bit of an expert at these

things, and, if you like, I can tell you how to a eat a tortoise."

Leopard stopped his scratching and his gnawing.

"Really?" he asked.

And Tortoise, still shivering inside his shell, asked himself the same question. "Really?" he wondered. "Is my friend Fox really going to tell the Leopard how to eat me?"

Fox cleared his throat. "Right, then," he began, "your problem is that the shell is too hard. What you need to do is to soften it up a bit. And what is better for softening things than water? So simply throw Tortoise into the river, wait for the shell to soften and then you will be able to eat him!"

Leopard was handsome and graceful and dangerous. But he was not very clever. So he did exactly what Fox suggested. He threw Tortoise into the river. Just as soon as Tortoise reached the bottom, he stretched out his legs and stuck out his head, and he sneaked silently away along the muddy river bed.

"How long do I wait?" asked Leopard, unaware that his dinner was long gone.

Fox looked up through the trees at the setting sun. "Until it is dark," he answered. "The darker the better!"

So Leopard waited by the river until midnight, growing hungrier and angrier as the night wore on, until he realized he never would have his dinner.

And as for Tortoise and Fox? The two friends had one more joke to laugh about together!

The Generous Rabbit

Rabbit shivered.

Rabbit sneezed.

The snow rose up to Rabbit's nose.

Rabbit rubbed her empty belly. Rabbit was hungry and tired and cold.

Then Rabbit stumbled across two turnips near the trunk of a tall pine tree.

So she hopped for joy, picked up the turnips and carried them all the way home.

Rabbit gobbled up the first turnip. But when she got to the second, she was full.

I bet my friend Donkey could use this turnip, Rabbit thought.

So she hopped all the way to Donkey's house, and, because Donkey was not at home, she left the turnip in Donkey's dish.

Donkey was looking for food as well.

Donkey shivered.

Donkey sneezed.

The snow rose up to Donkey's knees.

Donkey rubbed his empty belly. He was tired and hungry and cold.

Then Donkey spied two potatoes, near a fence in the farmer's field.

So he gave a happy "hee-haw", picked up the potatoes and carried them home.

Donkey gobbled up both potatoes, and then he noticed that a turnip had mysteriously appeared in his dish.

Now how did that get there? Donkey wondered. And being much too full to eat it, Donkey thought of his friend Sheep.

64

So Donkey carried the turnip to Sheep's house and, because Sheep was not at home, Donkey left the turnip on Sheep's soft bed of straw.

Sheep was looking for food as well.

Sheep shivered.

Sheep sneezed.

The snow rose up to Sheep's woolly tail.

Sheep rubbed her empty belly. She was tired and hungry and cold.

Then Sheep spotted a cabbage in the shadow of a snow-covered bush.

So she bleated a happy "Hooray!" and picked up the cabbage and carried it home.

Sheep gobbled up the cabbage. And then she noticed that a turnip had mysteriously appeared on her bed.

Now how did that get there? Sheep wondered. And, being much too full to eat it, she thought of her friend Squirrel.

So Sheep carried the turnip to Squirrel's house. And because Squirrel was not at home, she shoved the turnip into Squirrel's tree-trunk hole.

Squirrel was looking for food as well. (Just like everyone else!)

Squirrel shivered.

Squirrel sneezed.

The snow rose right up to Squirrel's ears.

Squirrel rubbed his empty belly. He was tired and hungry and cold.

And then Squirrel sniffed out a few nuts buried deep in the snowy soil.

Squirrel was so excited that he shook his bushy tail.

65

Then he carried the nuts back to his house.

When he got there, however, he couldn't get in. Someone had shoved a turnip into his tree-trunk hole!

Now how did that get there? Squirrel wondered. And, as he gobbled up the nuts, he thought of a friend, a friend who could surely use something to eat.

So he pulled the turnip out of the hole and pushed it through the snow, all the way… to Rabbit's house!

Rabbit was asleep, so Squirrel left the turnip by her side and crept quietly back home.

When Rabbit awoke, she was no longer tired, she was no longer cold. But she was hungry again.

I wish I'd kept that extra turnip, she thought. And when she opened her eyes, there it was, right beside her!

Now how did that get here? Rabbit wondered. Then she gobbled it up until she was full.

The Noble Rooster

Rooster was never on time.
   His job was simple enough, really.
   Wake up early.
   Watch for the sun.
   And then cry "Cock-a-doodle-do".
   But Rooster couldn't seem to get the hang of it.
   He didn't like waking up early.
   He fell asleep as he watched for the sun.
   And that's why his "Cock-a-doodle-dos" were always late.

The other chickens never let him forget it. They clucked and cackled and flapped their disapproval as he picked his way down from the barn roof each day. And that's what he thought they were doing, one particularly bright and sunny morning.

"Sorry," he muttered.

"Late again, I know," he yawned.

"Won't happen next time," he promised.

But no one paid any attention to him. And finally, he realized that they weren't talking about him at all.

"Haven't you heard?" clucked a big brown hen. "The ogre who lives on top of the mountain has been stomping all over the farmer's crops! And he has told the farmer that the only way he will stop is if the farmer promises to give him a chicken to eat, each and every day!"

"The farmer has challenged the ogre to a contest," clucked a little yellow chick. "If the ogre can build a stairway up the mountainside in just one night, the farmer will do what he asks. But if he cannot, the ogre will leave us all in peace."

"And that's where you come in, Rooster," clucked a third chicken. "The farmer and the ogre have agreed that the contest will come to an end when the sun rises and the rooster crows. We don't want the ogre to have any more time than necessary, which means that, for once, just once, you must not be late!"

Rooster wanted to say, "I can't do it."

He wanted to beg, "Find someone else."

He wanted to shout, "No, anyone but me!"

But one look at the chickens convinced him. They were counting on him. And he was determined, this time, not to let them down.

That very night, as the sun fell behind the barn, the contest began. The chickens watched nervously as the ogre picked up the first stone step and put it in place. He was gruesome, grumpy and green. He had one horrible horn sticking out the top of his head. And he was very, very strong. But it was a long way up the mountainside, so all the hens could do was hope as, one by one, they dropped off to sleep.

Rooster, meanwhile, was hiding in a corner of the farmyard. He knew he could never wake up on time. He knew that everyone was counting on him. So he decided not to go to sleep at all. And that way, he would be sure to greet the rising sun.

He walked round and round.

He jumped up and down.

He sang little songs and played little games and splashed his face again and again with cold water. He kept himself so busy, in fact, that he did not notice when that clever ogre sneaked into the farmyard. He did not see when that clever ogre slipped a little brown hood over the head of every sleeping chicken. And he did not hear when that clever ogre chuckled quietly to himself, "Now there will be no one to crow at the rising of the sun, and I'll be sure to win!"

But there was someone left to crow – someone whose eyelids grew heavy, whose head kept dropping on his feathery chest, but who kept awake as the stone stairway grew, step by step.

And as the first ray of morning sun crept up over the edge of the hills…

And as the ogre picked up the final stone…

And as he reared back his horrible head to laugh at his clever trick and celebrate his victory with a shout, Rooster staggered to his feet and cried, "Cock-a-doodle-do!"

It was a sleepy cock-a-doodle-do.

And it was a quiet cock-a-doodle-do.

But it was a cock-a-doodle-do nonetheless.

A cock-a-doodle-do that woke the farmer and the chickens and made the ogre howl, "Nooooo!"

The farmer was delighted.

The chickens were puzzled. Why is it still dark? they wondered.

And the ogre just dropped the last stone and walked over the mountain, dejected – never to be seen again.

There was a great celebration, of course. In the farmhouse. And in the farmyard too! And even though Rooster never again managed to cry "cock-a-doodle-do" on time, no one ever complained. Because he had done his best when it really mattered.

Rabbit and the Crops

Rabbit needed to feed his family.

Rabbit wanted to grow some food.

But Rabbit didn't have any land.

So he went to Bear, who had acres and acres of it, and asked if he could use a little piece.

"No problem," said Bear, "just as long as you give me a share of everything you grow."

"What share would you like?" asked Rabbit.

Bear just grinned. "My share will be everything that grows on top of the ground. And you can keep anything that grows underneath."

Rabbit thought about this for a minute. Then he shook Bear's big brown paw. "You have a deal!" he said.

71

And Bear just grinned some more. For now he would get everything that Rabbit grew, and Rabbit would be left with nothing but the roots!

Rabbit, however, knew exactly what he was doing. He called his children together. He told them to plant the field. And a few months later, when the crops were grown, he invited Bear down to collect his share.

"Now let me get this straight," said Rabbit, as they walked together to the field. "You get what's on top of the ground? And I get what's underneath?"

"That's the deal!" Bear grinned.

So Rabbit hollered to his children, "All right then, you can dig up those potatoes!"

And the grin slipped right off Bear's brown face. For now Rabbit would get all the potatoes, and Bear would be left with nothing but the useless potato plants!

The next year, Rabbit visited Bear again.

"I'd like to plant more crops on that piece of land," he said.

Bear just grinned. He wasn't going to be fooled this time. So he reached out his big brown paw and said, "No problem. But this year, I'll take what's on the bottom, and you can have what's on top!"

Rabbit thought about this for a minute, then shook Bear's big brown paw. "It's a deal," he said. And he and his children planted the field.

72

A few months later, when the crops were grown, Bear came to collect his potatoes.

But all he found waiting for him was a big pile of useless straw!

"Didn't I tell you?" said Rabbit. "I decided to plant oats this year. I've cut what I need right off the top and, as we agreed, the rest is yours!"

Bear was furious. But he did not let it show. No, he stomped home, planning hard how to get even with Rabbit.

The next year, Rabbit came to visit again. But before he could even ask, Bear had his answer ready.

"No problem!" he grinned. "Of course you can plant crops in my field again. But this year, I want the tops AND the bottoms for my share!"

Rabbit thought about this for a minute. Then he held out his paw. "It's a deal!" he grinned, and went off to plant the field.

Bear was so excited about his plan that he could hardly wait for the plants to grow. So he visited Rabbit a week or two before harvest, just to see how the crops were doing.

Rabbit welcomed him and led him to the field. But when Bear saw what was growing there, all he could do was let out a big bear groan, for Rabbit had tricked him again.

"As we agreed," grinned Rabbit, "you can have the tops AND the bottoms. And I'll keep the sweetcorn – that's growing in the MIDDLE!"

The Woman and the Bird

Whack! Whack! Whack! The woman hacked
at a banana tree.

High above, in the banana tree branches,
a mother bird sat on her nest.

"Stop it!" she begged. "Please stop it at
once!"

But all the woman could hear were the cries
of some noisy bird.

So – Whack! Whack! Whack! – she kept on hacking,
until finally the banana tree fell to the ground, taking
the poor bird's nest along with it.

"You've wrecked my nest! You've broken my eggs!"
cried the bird.

But all the woman could hear was screeching
and squawking, so she slung the axe over her
shoulder and headed home.

It wasn't long before the woman
had a baby of her own, and the
family was invited round to
celebrate his birth. Pure spring
water was needed for the naming
ceremony, so the woman sent
two of her little cousins, a boy
and a girl, off into the jungle to
fetch it.

When they got to the spring,
there in a tree, right in
front of them, sat the
mother bird. She was
the most beautiful
bird they had ever
seen, with a tail
like a jewelled

fan and a crown of feathers
on top of her head.

As they watched, the bird
began to dance.

She hopped back and forth.
She bobbed her head up and
down. She shook her feathery tail.
She turned round and round and round.
And as she danced, she sang a little song:

Watch me dance,
Hear me sing,
Stay with me
At the freshwater spring.

And so the children stayed. In fact, they could do nothing
else, for with her dancing and her singing the bird had put
them into a kind of a trance!

It wasn't long before the woman wondered where the
children had gone. So she sent her brother to look for them. He
found them at the spring. But, when he saw the beautiful bird
and heard her song, he too fell into a trance and could not move.

One by one, the woman sent all her relatives to the spring. And, one by one, they were entranced by the bird and failed to return. Finally, there was no one left at the house but the woman and her baby. So she made sure that he was bundled up safely, fast asleep in his bed, and she went off into the jungle as well.

As soon as the bird saw the woman, she stopped her dancing and her singing and flew out of the tree. And all at once, the cousins and the brothers and the sisters and the nieces and the nephews and the uncles and the aunts came to their senses.

"What have you been doing?" the woman shouted.

But all any of them could remember was the bird and her dance and her song.

Frustrated, the woman got some water from the spring, then led her relatives back towards the house. But as they got near, each and every one of them heard the baby cry. They rushed to the house, and there was the bird, high on the roof, with the baby in its claws!

"Please!" cried the woman. "Do not hurt my baby! Give him back to me, please!"

The bird did not sing. The bird did not dance. No, the bird simply spoke. And because the woman was paying attention this time, she understood exactly what the bird had to say.

"I begged you not to cut down my tree," said the bird. "I begged you to

spare my nest. I begged you not to destroy my precious eggs, just as you are begging me now. But you would not listen."

"I'm listening now!" the woman cried. "What do you want me to do?"

"I want you to understand," explained the bird, "that we creatures have feelings too – birds and beasts, everything that flies or crawls or roams through the jungle. We love our homes and we love our children, just as you do. And we cannot bear to watch you destroy them."

"I understand now. I really do," called the woman. "And I promise that I will always be kind to the creatures in the jungle. But please give me back my baby. I beg you!"

The bird rose from the roof, and it looked, for a moment, as if she might fly away. But then she floated down to the woman and laid the baby at her feet.

"Thank you," the woman sobbed, as she picked up her baby and cradled him in her arms.

Then the bird spread her wings and rose into the sky. And as she flew away, she sang another song:

Watch me dance.
Hear me sing.
Be at peace
With every living thing!

The Mole's Bridegroom

The Mole Lord had a lovely mole daughter. When the time came for her to marry, he decided that she should wed nothing less than the greatest thing in all the world. So he called together the wisest moles in Japan to help him find her a husband.

The moles scratched their thin mole beards and squinted their weak mole eyes. They thought very hard. And, at last, one mole stood and spoke.

"Surely, the greatest thing in all the world," he said, "is the sun."

"That's the answer then!" exclaimed the Mole Lord. "My daughter shall marry the sun!"

"Wait just a minute," said another mole, rising to his pale mole feet. "The sun may be great. But, all around the sun, we see the sky. So, surely, that is the greatest thing in all the world."

"So be it!" declared the Mole Lord. "My daughter shall marry the sky!"

"Not so fast," said yet another mole, tapping his long mole nose. "The sky is sometimes covered by clouds. So, surely, a cloud is the greatest thing in all the world."

"Excellent!" shouted the Mole Lord. "My daughter shall marry a cloud!"

"Wait," sighed another mole, scratching his smooth mole head. "Am I not right in saying that a strong wind can blow away any cloud? So, surely, the wind must be the greatest thing in all the world!"

"Brilliant!" grinned the Mole Lord. "My daughter shall marry the wind!"

"But no matter how hard the wind blows," suggested yet another mole, "it cannot move the earth! So, surely, the earth is the greatest thing in all the world!"

"Then it's settled," declared the Mole Lord. "My daughter shall marry the earth!"

"Yes, yes, yes," muttered the oldest, greyest and wisest mole of them all. "The earth may be hard. The earth may be strong. But what can dig a hole in the earth? A mole – that's what! And so I say, surely, a mole is the greatest thing in all the world."

"Why didn't I think of that?" asked the Mole Lord. "It's so obvious!"

And that is how the daughter of the Mole Lord came to marry… a mole!

The Kind-hearted Crocodile

"So what did you boys do today?" Mama Croc asked her croc-lings.

"I ate a dingo!" shouted Colin Croc.

"I ate a dingo and his mum!" boasted his brother Clive.

And then Mama Croc turned to her youngest boy and sighed. She had tried to bring up her boys in the best Croc tradition. But, in spite of all her talk about munching and crunching and gobbling up, young Christopher had still turned out to be the kindest croc in the county!

"Well," muttered Christopher, "I found a dingo too."

"Yes?" asked Mama Croc hopefully.

"And he was crying," said Christopher.

"Because you were so big and nasty?" added Mama Croc.

"No..." hesitated Christopher. "Because he was little and scared and somebody had just eaten his brother and his mum..."

"So I pulled out my hankie and wiped his eyes and took him by the paw and helped him find his dad."

Mama Croc wept into her apron.

The Croc brothers sniggered in the corner.

And Papa Croc looked over his paper and said much the same thing he said every night.

"Go to your room! And tonight, I want you to write DINGOS ARE FOR DINNER one hundred times, before you go to bed!"

The following evening, Mama Croc tried again.

"So what did you boys do today?" she asked.

"I ate a 'roo!" shouted Colin Croc.

"I ate a 'roo and his nephew!" boasted his brother Clive.

And then it was Christopher's turn.

"Well," he muttered. "I found a 'roo too."

"Yes...?" asked Mama Croc, crossing her fingers.

"And I would have eaten it and all its nieces and nephews, except..."

"Except the Croc Hunter came along and interrupted you?" hoped Mama Croc.

"Except a gigantic tidal wave swept you away?" giggled Colin Croc.

"Except you forgot your knife and fork?" suggested Clive Croc.

"Except the 'roo stubbed his big toe and you felt sorry for him," sighed Papa Croc.

"How did you guess?" moaned Christopher Croc. "And there were big tears in his eyes, as well, so I fished a plaster out of my rucksack and helped him home and had a very nice cup of tea with his gran."

Mama Croc sobbed into a towel.

The Croc brothers howled with laughter.

And Papa Croc just pointed upstairs.

"ROOS ARE FOR STEWS," he grunted. "Two hundred times. We'll see you in the morning."

It went the same way the rest of the week, as well.

"KOALAS ARE FOR KEBABING."

"GOANNAS ARE FOR GARNISHING."

"PLATYPUSES ARE FOR PICKLING."

So when Saturday arrived, Christopher Croc was determined to be anything but kind. He went out early, before anyone else was up, in search of something to frighten.

And, not two minutes later, the Croc Hunter sneaked into the house, surprised the sleeping Croc family, and bundled them all into his truck!

Christopher, meanwhile, was having no luck at all.

He growled at a 'roo.

81

"Nice to see you, Christopher!" she smiled.

He snapped at a platypus.

"And a good morning to you!" the platypus chirped.

He opened his mouth wide in the path of a baby bunny.

And the bunny just bounced on his tongue, laughing!

"I'll never be nasty!" he sighed. And because he was staring sadly at the ground, he walked right into the side of a house. The house of the Crocodile Hunter!

The Crocodile Hunter was every croc's enemy. This was the perfect chance to do something really nasty.

I could wreck the place! thought Christopher Croc. And teach that Crocodile Hunter a lesson!

But when he went inside, it looked as if it had already been wrecked! There were half-eaten tins of food lying about, dirty clothes everywhere, and there was dust on all the furniture.

There was no way that Christopher Croc could make that house any worse. But, as he looked around, he could think of all kinds of ways to make it better!

So he found an old broom and a crusty mop and set to work.

He washed and he scrubbed and he tidied. He even found a picture of the Croc Hunter's mum, buried under a pile of dirty dishes. So he cleaned it up and left it on the table, beside a little bunch of wild flowers. And just as he was finished, the truck pulled up outside.

There was nowhere to run, so Christopher Croc climbed into a cupboard.

Then he opened the door, just a crack, to see the hunter's reaction.

He thought the hunter might be surprised.

He hoped he would be pleased.

But he never expected what he actually saw – his entire family, tied up and gagged, at the end of the hunter's big rope!

If there was ever a time to be nasty – this was it! But before

Christopher Croc could leap out of the cupboard, the Crocodile Hunter began to sob.

He was staring at the picture of his mum – holding it between his trembling hands.

"I've missed you, Mum. I really have. I've been out in the swamps too long. And, by gum, I'm coming to see you. Not tomorrow. Not next week. But today. These Crocs'll keep. Your Billy Boy is coming home!"

And with that he scooped up the flowers, stuffed the picture inside his shirt, and ran out of the door.

When Christopher Croc heard the truck leave, he burst out of the cupboard and untied his family. At first, they were surprised to see him, and then they took a good look around the room.

"Been doing some cleaning?" asked Colin Croc.

"And some washing?" asked his brother Clive.

Christopher Croc looked at the floor. "Well…" he began.

"Well, good on ya! I say," shouted Papa Croc. "It looks like you've saved the day!"

So the Croc family headed home. And that night, the older Croc brothers had to write, three hundred times:

IT'S ALL RIGHT FOR A CROC TO BE KIND EVERY NOW AND THEN – WELL, AT LEAST WHEN YOUR FAMILY HAS BEEN CAUGHT BY A HUNTER WHO HASN'T SEEN HIS MUM FOR A WHILE.

Why the Tortoise Has No Hair

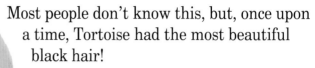

Most people don't know this, but, once upon a time, Tortoise had the most beautiful black hair!

Sometimes he would wear it piled high, in a big bouncy bouffant.

Sometimes he would comb it back, with a handful of grease – all Elvis-like.

And sometimes he would let it grow long, all the way down to his hard shell shoulders.

Tortoise loved his hair. In fact, the only thing he loved more was his breakfast.

One night, Tortoise stopped over at his mother-in-law's house. And when he stuck his head out of his shell the next morning, he smelled something that made his tortoise tummy rumble, and his thin tortoise lips dribble and drool. It was porridge – a huge hot steaming pot of porridge – bubbling away in the kitchen below.

Now, you may not like porridge. You may well be disgusted by its lumpy, gooey stickiness. But Tortoise adored porridge! Not Scottish-style porridge – savoury with butter and salt. And not American-style porridge, either – sweet with raisins and dark brown sugar. No, Tortoise adored Tortoise-style porridge – crunchy with river bugs and the odd muddy reed!

So Tortoise hurried down to breakfast. But not before he took a moment to organize his beautiful black hair. There was no time for a bouffant, and he had run out of grease, so he piled it all on top of his head, held it tight with a couple

84

of fancy clips, and then stuffed it under a big floppy hat.

"I'll put it up later," he promised himself. "In a nice pony-tail, perhaps!" Then he made his way to the table.

Did Tortoise say "Good Morning!" to anyone?

Did he ask how they had slept?

Did he take a second to bow his head and offer up a prayer of thanks?

No, he did not! Tortoise simply grabbed his bowl and sucked that porridge down in one long sickening slurp – muddy reeds and river bugs and all!

And then, of course, Tortoise was hungry for more. Not just some of the rest – but all of it!

So he made an excuse – "Oh dear, I've smeared a bit of river bug on my shell!" – and then ducked out into the kitchen as if to wipe it off. But once he got there, Tortoise went straight for the steaming hot porridge pot.

He would have gobbled it all down, right there and then, but he heard someone else coming towards the kitchen.

"Let me help you!" called his mother-in-law. "We don't want that river bug to stain!"

Tortoise panicked. He desperately wanted what was left of the porridge. But he was running out of time. So he dumped the porridge into his big floppy hat and, just as his mother-in-law came through the kitchen door, he plopped it back on his head!

"Oh, I see you've wiped it off already," said his mother-in-law. "And no stains at all. Excellent! Now come back to the table. There are a few things I need to ask you."

Tortoise staggered back to the table – his head boiling! He wanted to leave just as fast as he could. But his mother-in-law went on and on with her questions. How was his wife? How were the children? How were the next-door neighbours?

Finally, when Tortoise could stand the heat no longer, he jumped up from his seat and bolted for the door.

"Really must go!" he apologized. "I'll explain later. Sorry to eat and run."

Then Tortoise hurried out of the house, down the street, and ducked into an alley. Alone at last, he tore the hat off his head.

The porridge was still there, floating with reeds and river bugs. But something else was floating in there too – every last bit of Tortoise's beautiful black hair!

Tortoise looked in the hat and sighed.

His porridge was ruined.

His hair was gone.

If only he hadn't been so greedy.

And that, so they say, is why tortoises are bald to this very day.

Big Jack, Little Jack and the Bird

Big Jack and Little Jack were sad. Their little farm was failing and all their crops were gone. They were very, very poor.

"We've got no money!" sighed Big Jack.

"And no food, either!" added Little Jack.

So they went down to the river to catch some fish.

But even the fish weren't biting. So Big Jack and Little Jack went home empty-handed.

"We've caught no fish!" sighed Big Jack.

"No fish at all," added Little Jack. "I wish we'd caught just one – then we could have had some supper."

And that's when they saw a bird – a great big beautiful bird – sitting on the roof of their little rundown house.

"That's the biggest bird I've ever seen!" said Big Jack.

"And the most beautiful!" added Little Jack.

"That's very kind," said the bird. Then he flapped his wings and flew quickly out of sight.

"I believe that bird just spoke to us," said Big Jack.

"I believe you're right," said Little Jack.

And before they could say anything else, the bird returned, with a great big fish in his beak. "I heard your wish," said the bird. "I have very good hearing! And I will happily bring you a fish every day, if you like. Just as long as you let me sleep on your roof."

"That would be very helpful," said Big Jack.

"Very helpful indeed!" agreed Little Jack.

And so every day, for the next month, the great big beautiful bird brought a

How the Rabbit Lost Its Tail

Way back when the world was young, Rabbit had a long white tail!

Sometimes it dragged on the ground behind him.

Sometimes it stood straight up in the air.

But all the time, it followed Rabbit wherever he went.

One day, Rabbit wanted to visit an island, far across the sea. He curled up his tail like a long white spring, and sat there on the beach, bouncing and thinking. But no matter how long he bounced or how hard he thought, Rabbit could not find a way to get across the water.

Then, a shark swam by. And suddenly, Rabbit had an idea. A sneaky idea, for Rabbit was quite a trickster.

"Excuse me, Shark," he called. "I was just sitting here, bouncing and thinking – and I wondered – how many friends does a shark have?"

"Friends?" Shark replied. "Hundreds and hundreds, I should think."

"I'm surprised!" said Rabbit. "I always thought that sharks were quite fierce and lonely creatures."

"A common mistake," Shark grinned, his bright white teeth gleaming in the sunlight.

"We're really very friendly, and only show our fierce side when something makes us angry. Let me show you."

And with that, Shark disappeared beneath the surface of the water. But, when he came up again, he was not alone. There were hundreds of sharks, grinning behind him, stretched out across the water, as far as Rabbit could see!

"I'm impressed!" said Rabbit. "So many friends! Would you mind if I counted them?"

"Of course not," grinned Shark. "Do what you like. It will only prove my point."

So Rabbit counted the sharks. He hopped onto their heads, one by one, counting them as he went.

He hopped on ten sharks and twenty sharks and thirty sharks.

He hopped on forty sharks and fifty sharks and sixty sharks.

He hopped on seventy sharks and eighty sharks and ninety sharks.

And when he had hopped onto a hundred sharks, Rabbit just kept hopping – until he had hopped on the heads of three hundred sharks.

And then, Rabbit hopped onto the island!

"So have I made my point?" asked Shark, who had been swimming alongside Rabbit, all the while.

"Absolutely!" Rabbit chuckled.

"Then what's so funny?" asked Shark.

Rabbit chuckled again. And then, because he found it impossible to keep a good trick to himself, he went on.

"Well, I really couldn't care less how many friends you have. I just needed a way to cross the sea!"

Then Rabbit turned to walk away from the beach, his long tail dancing behind him. But Shark did not turn away. No, he did not like being tricked and was angry at Rabbit for making a fool of him and his friends. So, as Rabbit turned, Shark leaped out of the water and, flashing his sharp teeth, bit off Rabbit's long white tail.

"Yowch!" cried Rabbit, running off into the woods – his tail now no more than a little white tuft of a thing.

But did that teach him a lesson? Did it cure Rabbit of his trickster ways? It did not.

For when it came time to leave the island, Rabbit sat on the beach again. And simply waited until he found a different kind of fish – a fish with more friends than teeth!

The Badger Teapot

The little badger bounced up and down the hillside. He rolled, he tumbled, he threw himself on the soft grass and stared into the sky. It was a beautiful spring day, and he was determined to enjoy every minute of it.

And then – sproing! – a hunter's noose, hidden in the grass, looped itself round his leg and held him fast. The little badger was trapped!

Ting-a-ling. Clang-clang. Plonkety-plonk. A poor tinker came tramping by, his pots and pans banging around on his back.

"Help me! Help me, please!" the badger cried. And the tinker felt so sorry for him that he untied the noose straightaway and set the badger free.

The badger bounced up and down again. "How can I ever repay you?" he asked the tinker. "I will do anything. Please tell me how."

"There is no need to repay me," smiled the tinker. "Run back to your home. Enjoy this lovely day. That is payment enough for me." And he tramped off again – Ting-a-ling, Clang-clang, Plonkety-plonk.

93

The badger, however, was determined to repay the tinker for his kindness. And just before the tinker had walked out of sight, he had an idea. He wiggled his badger nose. He shut his badger eyes. He shook his badger body. He wished really hard. And he turned himself into a teapot! How he did it, he didn't quite know, but there he was – a beautiful badger teapot, covered in delicate black and white patterns, with a badger tail for a handle, and a badger nose for a spout, and four porcelain badger feet.

Then he ran off after the tinker. And without the tinker knowing it, he leaped onto the pile of pots and pans on the tinker's back and held tight – Ting-a-ling, Clang-clang, Plonkety-plonk – all the way back to the tinker's house.

When the tinker unloaded his pots and pans, he was surprised to find the teapot among them.

"Where did this come from?" asked his wife.

"I don't know," said the tinker. "But it's very nice, isn't it? Why don't you make us some tea?"

And so the tinker's wife did. She set the teapot on the table. She boiled some water. She poured it into the pot. And then – oh my! – the beautiful teapot

began to bounce around the room!

"Hot! Hot! Much too hot!" the teapot shrieked. So the tinker's wife picked it up and emptied it and called for her husband, the tinker.

"There's a ghost in this teapot!" she complained. "You must take it back to wherever you found it!"

"No! No!" the teapot cried. "I am not a ghost. I am the little badger you rescued on the hillside. I turned myself into a teapot to repay you."

"You're not much help, then," moaned the tinker's wife. "What good is a teapot that can't hold hot water?"

"I'll tell you what," said the teapot. "I'm still a badger at heart. I can tumble and balance and dance. Why not put on a little circus? And I will be your star!"

"I could make the curtains," offered the tinker's wife.

"And I could build a little stage," said the tinker. "Yes, why not! Thank you Badger Teapot."

So they sewed curtains and built a stage and put notices all around the village: "Come and see the Amazing Tumbling Teapot."

People were curious, of course, and paid good money to see this Tumbling Teapot. And they were not disappointed. The teapot did somersaults. The teapot did backflips. And, most impressive of all, the teapot walked across a tightrope, holding a bright red parasol in his snout – or rather – spout!

The people clapped. The people cheered. The people came from miles around. And soon the tinker was a very rich man indeed.

"You have repaid me more than I deserve," he said to the teapot, one day. "I think it is time you went back to your home."

"That is very kind," said the teapot. And with a wiggle and a wink and a shake and a wish, he turned himself back into a badger. How he did it, he didn't quite know, but when he had finished, the badger said goodbye and tumbled back to the hillside.

And the tinker and his wife and the badger, who was no longer a teapot, lived happily ever after.

The Kind of Hungry Lion

Once there was a kind of hungry lion, whose stomach growled softly, like a little lion cub.

The kind of hungry lion went to look for something to eat. He peeped around a boulder and saw a family of rock badgers having a picnic.

I'm not hungry enough to eat a whole rock badger, thought the kind of hungry lion. But half a badger would make a very nice snack.

Just then, his stomach growled again, louder this time, and the badgers looked his way.

"Look!" shouted a little brown rock badger. "A lion has come to our picnic!"

"Don't be shy," called the badger's wife. "Come along and join us!"

The kind of hungry lion didn't know what to think. But then his stomach growled a little louder. So he decided that he would join the badgers' picnic. And if he got tired of that, he could always picnic on the badgers!

The badgers brought the lion a deck chair and a little table. Then they poured him a glass of lemonade, with four ice cubes and a bendy straw!

Soon someone called, "Supper!" and all the badgers ran into a tall tent. By now, the kind of hungry lion had

96

become a hungry lion, and his stomach's growl was as loud as his own.

The rock badgers gave him the best seat and piled plates of pretty sandwiches in front of him. A toothpick, with a little sign, had been stuck into the top sandwich on each plate.

Everyone looked at the hungry lion. And the hungry lion looked at the little signs.

"Parsley" said the first sign. And the lion gagged. Even really hungry lions didn't eat parsley.

"Cress" said the second sign. And the lion gagged again. Even very hungry lions didn't eat cress.

There was only one sign left. The lion swallowed hard and then read it. "Clover" is what it said. And the lion thought he would cry.

What could he do? He was a hungry lion. But lions don't eat parsley and cress and clover. Lions eat meat! Like antelopes and buffaloes and… rock badgers.

But the rock badgers had been so kind to him. How could he eat them and spoil their lovely picnic?

And

that's when the hungry lion smelled something.
"What's that?" he asked.

The little brown rock badger sniffed the air. "It smells like something cooking," he said. "The jackals are having a picnic over the ridge. Perhaps the smell is coming from there."

The hungry lion stood up so fast he nearly poked his head through the top of the tent. "I'm very sorry," he apologized. "I have to go now. Thank you for a lovely afternoon." And with that, the hungry lion dashed off after that wonderful smell. He was a very hungry lion now, and his stomach was roaring as only a lion's stomach can.

What could they be cooking? he wondered. Antelope? Camel? Elephant stew? And then he reached the jackals' picnic and just stood and stared at the fattest, juiciest ox he had ever seen! Two jackals were turning it on a spit and splashing it with barbecue sauce.

"Excuse me," asked the very hungry lion. "Could I join you for dinner?"

The jackals didn't smile or say "Hello". They didn't even look at him.

"Get in the queue!" barked one of the jackals. "Over by the table."

The lion took his roaring stomach over to the end of the queue. The jackals were pushing and shoving one another, and, before he knew it, the very hungry lion was being pushed and shoved too. There were jackal elbows in his back and jackal knees up his nose, but at last he crawled out of that jumble with a knife and a fork and a plate – and a thick, juicy ox steak!

He sat down at the table, but before he could pick up his knife, an old grey jackal spat and hollered, "That's MY seat! I've been coming to jackal picnics for fifty years, and I ALWAYS sit there!"

The very hungry lion picked up his plate and found himself between two angry lady jackals. They were snapping and snarling and waving their handbags and, before the lion could move, one of the handbags slammed against his plate and sent it flying. And the very hungry lion watched his steak fall flat onto the ground!

The lion bent down and picked up his steak. His dinner was now a brown muddy mess. "You know what you are?" he roared. "You're nothing but a bunch of ANIMALS!" Then he stomped out of the clearing and back over the ridge.

Now a very, very hungry lion, he stomped right back to the badgers' picnic, straight into their big tent.

And then there was a roar, a roar so loud and fierce that all the other animals stopped their picnics to listen. The roar was followed by the sound of running feet, overturned tables and broken plates. And, finally, everything went quiet.

The other animals spent a sad moment thinking about the poor rock badgers and how they had ended up as part of the lion's dinner.

Meanwhile, inside the tent, the very full and happy lion leaned back in his chair and licked the tips of his claws.

"I've never heard a stomach growl so loudly in all my life," said the little brown rock badger. "I'm just glad we had more sandwiches. But I'm sorry we made such a noise and fuss getting it all together."

"Just as long as our guest enjoyed himself," smiled the badger's wife. "And by the looks of him, I'd say he did. Can we get you anything else?" she asked the lion.

The lion patted his quiet tummy. "Yes please," he smiled. "I think I've got room for just one more of those clover sandwiches."

The Big, Soft, Fluffy Bed

Granny put Danny to bed – in her big, soft, fluffy bed.

But when she closed the door behind her – closed it ever so slowly and ever so gently – the hinge on the door went Squeeeek!

And Danny woke up with a cry!

"Oh dear," said Granny, "I know what we'll do. We'll let the kitten sleep with you, just this once. And she can keep you company!"

So Granny put Danny to bed again – in her big, soft, fluffy bed.

With the kitten curled up at his feet.

But when she closed the door – closed it ever so slowly and ever so gently – the hinge on the door went Squeeeek!

Danny woke up with a cry!

And the kitten jumped up with a "Miaow!"

"Oh dear," said Granny, "I know what we'll do. We'll let the dog sleep with you, just this once. He can keep you company!"

So Granny put Danny to bed again – in her big, soft, fluffy bed.

With the kitten curled up at his feet.

And the dog stretched out beside him.

But when she closed the door – closed it ever so slowly and ever so gently – the hinge on the door went Squeeeek!

Danny woke up with a cry!

The kitten jumped up with a "Miaow!"

And the dog leaped up with a "Woof!"

"Oh dear," said Granny, "I know what we'll do. We'll let the pig sleep with you, just this once. She can keep you company!"

So Granny put Danny to bed again – in her big, soft, fluffy bed.

With the kitten curled up at his feet.

And the dog stretched out beside him.

And the pig right next to his pillow.

But when she closed the door – closed it ever so slowly and ever so gently – the hinge on the door went Squeeek!

Danny woke up with a cry!

The kitten jumped up with a "Miaow!"

The dog leaped up with a "Woof!"

And the pig rolled over with an "Oink!"

"Oh dear," said Granny, "I know what we'll do. We'll let the pony sleep with you, just this once, and he can keep you company!"

So Granny put Danny to bed again – in her big, soft, fluffy bed.

With the kitten curled up at his feet.

And the dog stretched out beside him.

And the pig right next to his pillow.

And the pony squeezed between them all!

But when she closed the door – closed it ever so slowly and ever so gently – the hinge on the door went Squeeeek!

Danny woke up with a cry!

The kitten jumped up with a "Miaow!"

The dog leaped up with a "Woof!"

The pig rolled over with an "Oink!"

The pony bounced up and down with a "Neigh!"
And the big, soft, fluffy bed fell down with a crash.
"Oh dear," said Granny, "this will never do!"
So she shooed the kitten back into the kitchen.
Walked the dog out into the yard.
Persuaded the pig to go back to her pigsty.
And led the pony to the barn.
Then Granny mended the big, soft, fluffy bed.
She looked at the door.
She looked at the rusty hinge.
And then she went out to the shed and came back with a little can of oil.
Granny squirted the oil on the hinge, then one last time, she put Danny
to bed – in the big, soft, fluffy bed.
And when she closed the door – closed it ever so slowly and ever so gently
– the hinge on the door… made no sound at all!
And Danny fell fast asleep.

The Peanut Boy

Henry and his dad were going fishing.

They packed their tackle and their bait. They slung their fishing rods over their shoulders. But just as they were about to leave for the river, Henry's mum asked Henry's dad to step into the kitchen.

Henry's mum and Henry's dad talked and talked and talked.

Henry waited and waited.

And when he got tired of waiting, he decided to do something just a little more interesting. He decided to turn himself into a peanut!

How he did it, nobody knew.

Where he learned it was a mystery.

But it was a talent – no question about that.

So Henry shut his eyes. Henry scrunched up his face. And, in a flash, Henry was a peanut, tucked up in a peanut shell.

He sat there for a while, all cosy and peanut-like. And then a chicken came clucking by. She saw the peanut lying on the ground, and, before Henry could turn himself back into a boy, she gobbled that peanut up.

So there was: Henry in a peanut shell.

Henry in a chicken.

And Henry's mum and Henry's dad just talking in the kitchen.

It wasn't long before a fox crept by. And, being a fox, he did what foxes do best. He swallowed down that chicken in one great big bite.

So there was: Henry in a peanut shell.

Henry in a chicken.

Henry in a sly old fox.

And Henry's mum and Henry's dad just talking in the kitchen.

The fox walked off into the woods. But it wasn't long before he met a wolf. The wolf was hungry. And even though he would have preferred a nice doe or a tasty rabbit, he wolfed down that fox until he could find something better.

So there was: Henry in a peanut shell.

Henry in a chicken.

Henry in a sly old fox.

Henry in a hungry wolf.

And Henry's mum and Henry's dad just talking in the kitchen.

The wolf was thirsty so he wandered on down to the river to get himself something to drink.

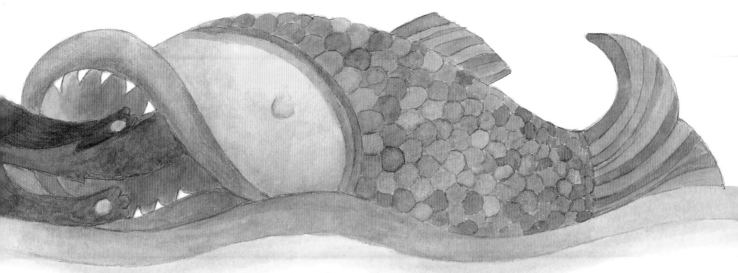

But when he dipped his tongue into the water, up sprang the biggest fish he had ever seen and gulped him down between its big, fat, fishy lips!

So there was: Henry in a peanut shell.

Henry in a chicken.

Henry in a sly old fox.

Henry in a hungry wolf.

Henry in a great big fish.

And Henry's mum and Henry's dad just talking in the kitchen.

At last the talking stopped.

Henry's mum had had her say. And Henry's dad had too. So he went out looking for Henry. His tackle and his bait and his fishing rod were right outside the kitchen door. But Henry was gone.

Probably tired of waiting, thought Henry's dad. So he went down to the river, alone.

He put the bait on his hook.

He tossed the line into the river.

And what took hold of that line was the biggest fish he had ever seen.

Henry's dad pulled and pulled and pulled. And, finally, he pulled that big fish right up onto the shore.

He reached his hand into the fish's mouth to fetch his hook – and out popped the wolf!

The wolf opened his mouth to howl – and out popped the fox!

The fox opened his mouth to catch his breath – and out popped the chicken!

105

The chicken sneezed – and out popped the peanut!

And as soon as Henry's dad saw the peanut, he nodded his head and he grinned. You see, he knew all about Henry's special talent. So he did what he always did when Henry hid himself in a peanut.

He picked up the peanut, tossed it in the air and said, as loudly as he could, "I think it's time to make some peanut butter!"

And, as soon as Henry heard that, he turned himself into a boy again. "I'm feeling a little hungry," said Henry's dad.

"Me too," said Henry.

So they picked up the fish and carried it home. And, as they fried it up in their very biggest pan, Henry told his mum and dad about everything that had happened:

Henry in a peanut shell.

Henry in a chicken.

Henry in a sly old fox.

Henry in a hungry wolf.

Henry in a great big fish.

Henry safe back home again.

And Henry's mum and Henry's dad just listening in the kitchen.

The Wonderful Bird

The three sisters worked hard in the fields. They planted and weeded and helped with the harvest, even though they were very young. But what else could they do? Their parents were dead. They were poor and hungry, and their greedy uncle would do nothing to help them.

One afternoon, as they were finishing their work, the three sisters stumbled across a wounded little bird. She fluttered and flapped and flopped about on the ground. They were sad to see her like this so they they picked her up carefully and carried her home. Then they made a little bird cage out of sticks and, day by day, nursed her back to health.

"Kekeko. Kekeko." That was the sound the little bird made when she was well again. So that's what the sisters named her – Kekeko.

One evening, just as the sisters were preparing for bed, Kekeko did something that surprised them. She did not stick her head under her wing. She did not say, "Kekeko." No, she looked straight at the sisters and she spoke!

"Let me sleep in your biggest basket tonight," chirped Kekeko. "And I will lay some food for you."

The three sisters stared at the bird. They were so shocked to hear her speak that they did just what she asked. But the next morning, when they awoke,

they were even more surprised. For Kekeko was back in her cage, and the basket was full of cooked fish and warm rice!

"See!" cried Kekeko. "I have laid for you! Put me in the basket again tonight, and I will do the same."

The hungry sisters did not stop to wonder how a bird could lay such food. They just gobbled down the fish and rice. They had never eaten so much! That night, Kekeko filled the basket again. And again and again, each night that followed.

Soon, Kekeko was laying so much fish and rice that the girls could not finish it.

"Would it be possible for you to lay uncooked rice instead?" asked the most sensible sister, at last. "That way we could store it, and perhaps pass it on to some of our poorer neighbours."

Kekeko was happy to oblige. She laid so much rice, in fact, that the girls had enough for themselves and all their poor friends. Word of their good fortune spread across the village. And that is when their greedy uncle came to visit.

"I understand you have a wonderful bird!" he said. "And that she lays you more rice than you can use. Would you mind if I took her home with me for a day or two?"

The sisters looked at one another. This was a hard decision. Their uncle had never shown them any kindness. But did that mean that they should refuse to be kind to him?

In the end, they agreed to let him borrow her. "We have more than enough to eat," they said. "We are happy to share our good fortune with you."

So the greedy uncle put Kekeko in her cage and carried her off to his house.

One day passed. And a second. And a third. The girls still had plenty to eat, but they were missing their little friend very much now. So they went to their uncle's house and knocked on his door.

"Excuse us," they said, "but could we have Kekeko back now?"

"I don't think so," said the greedy uncle.

"Why?" asked one of the sisters. "Because you want her to lay more rice?"

"No," the uncle scowled. "Because I have eaten her!"

At once, the three sisters burst into tears.

"Stop your blubbering!" the uncle shouted. "The silly bird deserved it! I put her in a basket two nights in a row – the biggest basket I could find. And did she give me any rice? Not a grain. All she did was chirp on and on about how I had neglected you. So I put an end to her chirping and had her for my breakfast. And a tiny breakfast it was, at that!"

Then the greedy uncle went into the kitchen, scooped up Kekeko's bones and gave them to the girls, along with her little birdcage.

"Here," he sneered. "See for yourselves. This is all that's left!"

The three sisters trudged home, weeping as they went. They had no thought for the future or for what they would do when the rice ran out. They thought only about poor little Kekeko.

So when they returned home, the first thing they did was to bury her. They put the bones in the bird cage. They put the cage in a hole. Then they covered the hole with dirt and laid the basket on the top. And, weeping still, they went to bed.

When they woke the next
morning, the three sisters went into the
garden to look at Kekeko's grave. But the grave was gone!
In its place stood a little tree, with broad leafy branches. And,
hanging on the branches, were silver rings and golden necklaces
and more shiny treasures than the girls had ever seen. The three
sisters would never be poor again!

But best of all, when the wind blew through the branches,
there came a sound – "Kekeko. Kekeko." And the sisters
knew that their little friend was with them still.

The Cat, the Mice and the Cheese

Once upon a time, there were two little mice who stumbled across one great big chunk of cheese.

"It's mine!" said the grey mouse. "I saw it first!"

"Yours?" cried the brown mouse. "I beg to differ, but I think it's mine!"

And they squeaked and scratched and squabbled for an hour or more.

"This is getting us nowhere," sighed the grey mouse, at last. "Why don't we just split it?"

"And I suppose you'll be the one who does the splitting," said the brown mouse. "I can see what you're up to."

"Well, I wouldn't want you to do it," sneered the grey mouse. "You'd be sure to cut yourself the bigger piece."

Suddenly, another voice joined the conversation. "Perhaps I can be of some help."

And when the mice turned around, there appeared a huge ginger cat!

There was no time to run. Nowhere to hide. So the mice just stood there, shivering with fear.

"There's nothing to be afraid of," grinned the cat. "I am here to help. You may not believe this, but I like a bit of cheese, myself, from time to time. So I understand your problem perfectly. Why not let *me* divide the cheese for you?"

The mice looked at each another. It seemed a reasonable solution. And, besides, they didn't have much choice.

"All right," said the grey mouse.

"As long as you're fair," added the brown mouse.

And the cat grinned again. Then he reached out one sharp claw and cut the cheese in two.

But as soon as he'd finished, it was clear that one piece was bigger than the other.

"The big piece is mine!" squeaked the grey mouse.

"Oh no it isn't!" squeaked the brown mouse in reply. And the argument started up again.

"I'm terribly sorry!" apologized the cat. "It seems that I have made things even worse. Here, let me put it right."

And he shaved a bit off the bigger piece – and popped it into his mouth!

"Mmm," said the cat. "Very nice. Very nice, indeed!"

"But it's still not right!" complained the grey mouse. "You shaved off too much. Now the other piece is bigger!"

"MY piece, you mean!" squeaked the brown mouse. "You didn't want it! Remember?"

"I want it now that it's bigger!" cried the grey mouse.

And the cat had to interrupt again.

"Now, now," he purred. "This is easily fixed." And again he shaved a bit off the bigger piece and popped it into his mouth!

"Creamy!" he mewed. "So thick and so rich."

But the mice were still not happy – not happy at all. For now the other piece was bigger again.

On and on went the arguing. And so did the shaving and the eating and the purring as, bit by bit, the cat gobbled up the cheese. Finally, there was nothing left, but one last bite.

"Wait a minute!" cried the grey mouse. "The cheese is almost gone!"

"That's right," cried the brown mouse. "So that last little piece is mine!"

"Oh no it's not!" squeaked the grey mouse.

And the cat just grinned again.

"I see what you mean," he said. "It's only a little piece, isn't it? Hardly worth fighting over."

And with that, he speared the cheese with his claw and popped it into his mouth!

The grey mouse and the brown mouse both gasped in horror!

"You've eaten it all!" they cried. "And we've had nothing!"

"Nothing but a good argument," said the cat. "And you might have had so much more, if only you had been a little less greedy and tried a little harder to get along."

"It's not fair!" squeaked the grey mouse. "You've cheated us."

"Careful," growled the cat. "I only did what I promised. If I were you, I'd be grateful that the cheese was not the only thing I gobbled down!"

Then he cleaned his claws and licked his lips and padded away.

And the grey mouse and the brown mouse trudged sadly home.

The Goats and the Hyena

Once upon a time, on a high and grassy hill, there lived three goats.

Siksik was the biggest.

Mikmik was almost as big.

And the smallest was Jureybon.

One day, the three goats went for a walk – through the rocky passes to a field on the next hill. They grazed all day and, as the sun began to set, they set off for home.

Siksik led the way – for he was the biggest.

Mikmik followed close behind – for he was almost as big.

And little Jureybon straggled far behind – for he was the smallest.

They squeezed past huge boulders and leaped over deep ravines. But as Siksik turned the very last corner, he found himself face to face with a very big and very hungry hyena!

"I have three questions for you, goat!" growled the hyena.

"Ask away, sir," Siksik trembled.

"What are those points on your head?" the hyena asked.

"They are my horns, sir," Siksik trembled.

"What is that patch on your back?"

"It is my woolly coat, sir."

"Then why are you shivering?" the hyena roared.

"Because I am afraid that you will eat me, sir," cried Siksik.

"For my dinner, I think!" the hyena drooled. Then, with one blow of his paw, he knocked Siksik down cold.

And, not a second later, Mikmik turned the corner.

"I have three questions for you, goat!" growled the hyena.

"Ask away, sir," Mikmik trembled.

"What are those points on your head?" the hyena asked.

"They are my horns, sir," Mikmik trembled.

"What is that patch on your back?"

"It is my woolly coat, sir."

"Then why are you shivering?" the hyena roared.

"Because I am afraid that you will eat me, sir," cried Mikmik.

"For my breakfast, I think!" the hyena drooled. And, with one blow of his paw, he knocked Mikmik out as well.

If Jureybon had been bigger, if Jureybon had been faster, if Jureybon had not been straggling behind, he too might have turned the corner a second later.

But he was the smallest goat, and the slowest – so he had time to come up with a plan!

He hid around the corner, so that the hyena could not see him. Then he called out in the deepest and angriest voice he could muster: "I have three questions for you, hyena!"

115

The hyena was confused. This was his line!

"Ask away, sir," the hyena growled.

"What are these points on my head?" asked Jureybon.

The hyena was even more confused. "Your horns?" he guessed.

"No, you fool!" roared Jureybon. "These are my two sharp swords!"

"Second question. What is this patch on my back?" Jureybon continued.

The hyena did not like this one bit. "Your woolly coat?" he trembled.

"Coat?" howled Jureybon. "Don't be ridiculous. This is my mighty shield!"

Shield? wondered the hyena. Swords? And he grew more nervous still.

"And finally!" growled Jureybon. "One last question. Why am I shivering?"

"Because you are afraid, sir?" the hyena shivered back.

"Because I am trembling with rage!!" roared Jureybon. "And cannot wait to come round this corner and knock you out!"

The hyena couldn't wait either – to get away! He forgot all about his breakfast and his dinner and ran all the way back to his cave.

Then Jureybon danced happily round the corner. He woke up Siksik. He woke up Mikmik. And the three goats went back to their high and grassy hill.

The Clever Crows

Big Crow and Little Crow were thirsty.

It had not rained for months. The world was like a desert. Everything was dry.

Then Big Crow spotted a bottle – a clear glass bottle – in a dark corner of a shady courtyard. And in the bottom of the bottle there was water! Not much water, but enough for both of them to have a drink.

Little Crow stuck his beak into the bottle. And, as soon as he did, he began to cry.

"The water's too far down!" he wept. "We'll never reach it."

"And if we tip the bottle over," sighed Big Crow in reply, "the water will soak into the dry ground before we have a chance to drink it."

But then Big Crow spotted a pebble – a shiny black pebble – in the middle of the courtyard. And Big Crow had an idea.

He hopped into the middle of the courtyard, picked up the pebble and hopped back into the shady corner.

Then he winked and said to Little Crow, "Watch this!"

With the pebble in his beak, he put his beak in the bottle. He dropped the pebble in the water, and the water rose higher!

Little Crow peered into the bottle.

"There's one pebble down there," he said. "But the water is still too low for me to reach."

"Then we will have to put in more," said Big Crow. And he picked up a silver pebble, and a bright white one too.

And, with the pebbles in his beak, he put his beak in the bottle. He dropped the pebbles in the water, and the water rose higher!

"One pebble. And two more pebbles. That makes three pebbles," said Little Crow. "And that's a lot better. But the water is still too low."

"Then we will add some more," said Big Crow. And he found a brown pebble and a green pebble and a white pebble.

And, with the pebbles in his beak, he put his beak in the bottle. He dropped the pebbles in the water, and the water rose higher!

"Three more pebbles," said Little Crow. "That makes six altogether. But the water is still too low. Can I drop the pebbles in this time?"

"Be my guest!" said Big Crow.

So Little Crow (who was very thirsty by now) found four pebbles – a red one, a purple one, a yellow one and a blue one.

And, with the pebbles in his beak, he put his beak in the bottle. He dropped the pebbles in the water, and the water rose higher!

"Six pebbles and four pebbles. That makes ten pebbles now!" said Big Crow. "I think we've finally done it!"

And so they had. For when Little Crow stuck his beak into the bottle, he could finally reach the water!

So Little Crow had a drink. And Big Crow did too. And then they flew away, leaving one glass bottle and ten shiny pebbles.

The Monkeys and the Mangoes

Once upon a time, at the edge of a mighty river, a little monkey found a mango tree.

He munched on the mango and – Mmm! – it was amazing. Sweet and juicy and more delicious than anything he had ever tasted.

The little monkey crossed the river and took the mango to the Monkey King. And when the Monkey King munched on the mango – Mmm! – he thought it was amazing too.

So the Monkey King, along with many more monkeys, made his way across the river to the mango tree.

The monkeys picked mangoes all morning and all afternoon, until it was night. Then they curled up in the branches of the mango tree and fell fast asleep. They had managed to eat many mangoes, but there were many more mangoes left. As they slept, one of those mangoes dropped from its branch into the mighty river, and floated downstream to the kingdom of men.

The next morning, as the King of Men was bathing in the river, the mango floated by. The king had never seen a mango before, but he thought it looked quite tasty. So he picked it up and handed it to one of his servants.

"Eat this!" he commanded. "Is it good? Is it bad? Is it poison? I need to know!"

So the servant munched on the mango and – Mmm! – it was amazing!

"The fruit is sweet and juicy!" he told the king. "More delicious than anything I have ever eaten!"

So the King of Men took a bite and – Mmm! – he thought it was amazing too!

"Call my soldiers!" he commanded. "We must travel up river and find more of this amazing fruit."

So the King of Men, his servants and his soldiers made their way to the mango tree. When the Monkey King saw them coming, he led the rest of the monkeys into the highest branches of the mango tree and told them to keep very, very still.

The servants picked mangoes all morning and all afternoon, and, just as it was turning dark, one of the soldiers spotted the tail of the little monkey, hanging down from the highest branch.

When he told the King of Men, the king just grinned.

"Roast monkey will go very nicely with this fruit," he said. "Take your bows and shoot the monkey down!"

Soon, arrows began to sail through the branches of the mango tree. The Monkey King knew that there was

120

only one thing to do. He was the biggest monkey of them all, so he leaped from the branches of the mango tree, across the mighty river, to a tree on the other side. Then he tied a long vine around one of his legs and leaped back across the river. He hoped to make a vine bridge so the monkeys could escape. But the vine was too short, and he could only make the bridge reach by stretching out his own body and holding onto the nearest mango branch.

So the Monkey King, himself, was now part of the bridge and he called for the monkeys to climb across his back to the other side.

"There are too many of us!" cried the little monkey. "We will break your back!"

"Just do as I say!" commanded the Monkey King.

So with the arrows flying all around, the monkeys climbed across their king's back to the safety of the farther shore.

The King of Men watched, amazed. Then he ordered his soldiers to put down their bows.

"Fetch me that monkey!" he commanded, pointing to the Monkey King. But, by the time the soldiers carried him down, the Monkey King was almost dead. For, as the little monkey had worried, the weight of the rest of the monkeys had broken his back.

The King of Men held the Monkey King in his arms and asked him one simple question: "Why? Why did you do it?"

The Monkey King's answer was more simple still.

"To save my people," he whispered. "For they are more important to me than any mango. More important than anything at all."

Then the Monkey King closed his eyes and died.

The King of Men looked at his own people – at his servants and at his soldiers. Then he ordered them to leave the mangoes and to follow him back to the kingdom of men. And there, in his own palace, the King of Men built a beautiful tomb for the Monkey King, so that he would never forget how a true king should act.

Sharing stories with a crowd

Storytelling was never meant to be a one-way street. At its best, it is a kind of dialogue, something that happens between a storyteller and his listeners. One way to encourage this in a larger group is to give your audience specific ways to participate in the story. Here are my suggestions for how to get groups of children (or adults) more involved in the stories from *The Lion Storyteller Book of Animal Tales*. It's all very simple, although sometimes you may need to spend a while teaching people how to say their lines.

Some of these suggestions will also work when you're sharing the stories with only one or two children (although you may not want to make bedtime reading *too* exciting). They may even spark off other storytelling ideas of your own.

The main thing is to have fun with the storytelling and if an idea doesn't work, try something else instead. Enjoy yourself – and your listeners will enjoy themselves too.

The Fox and the Crow

You play the fox and have your crowd play the crow, scratching their heads when she is confused, smiling when she is flattered, trembling when she does, but all the while keeping their mouths shut very tightly. Then have the crowd let out an awful "squawk" when crow tries to sing.

City Mouse and Country Mouse

Have everyone make car sounds, and maybe even turn a pretend steering wheel. Have them go "beep-beep" when Mouse's car is moving through town, then a quiet "humm" when it goes a little more quickly in the suburbs, then a throaty "roar" when Mouse speeds through the country.

You can also divide them into three groups – one to make cat sounds, one to make dog sounds, and one to make the "snap" of the mouse trap.

Why the Cat Falls on Her Feet

Make this a counting story. Teach everyone the numbers and the sounds ahead of time.

When Eagle is mentioned, have everyone hold up two fingers and "screech". For Snake, have everyone make a "zero" with their thumb and forefinger and "hiss". Spider – eight fingers and a "scrickety-scrackety" sound. Possum – one finger and a big yawn. Ant – six fingers and a grunt. Cat – four fingers in a claw shape and a noisy "meow".

Big Jack, Little Jack and the Donkey

Have everyone say "That is the silliest thing I ever saw!" in five different voices – the old woman, the old man, the girl, the boy, and the mayor. Teach them the voices ahead of time.

As an option, you might divide the crowd into five groups, one for each of the voices.

The Lion's Advice

Have your group play the lion, roaring, growling, and sniffing when he does.

The Dog and the Wolf

Have everyone play the dog. Growl when he growls. Gobble up the dog food with him (maybe a big "Mmm" at the end!). Curl up and fall to sleep with him (doggy snores). Lie in front of the fireplace (contented doggy sighs). And maybe lots of panting and happy yipping when he talks about playing with the farmer. But when the dog mentions the collar, have everyone tug at their collars. And when he mentions the chain, have everyone try to move and get jerked back.

Practice the motions and sounds ahead of time.

The Kind Parrot

Have everyone say the first line of the "parrot poems" with you in a squawky parrot voice.

The Tortoise and the Hare

Divide your group into two. Have one half play the hare – hands for ears, buck-toothed, and beating the floor with their feet every time hare runs. Have the other half play the tortoise – jumpers and tops pulled up under their noses for shells, and moving their hands and feet very very slowly.

If you'd rather not pitch them against each other, you can also have everyone play the tortoise and the hare!

Why Dogs Chase Cats and Cats Chase Mice

Divide your group into three – dogs, cats, and mice. Have the dog group do what the dogs do in the story – woofing, yipping, yapping, wagging tales, scratching, and barking. Have the cat group stretch and meow and purr. And have the mice group nibble and nibble and nibble!

Rabbit and the Briar Patch

Have everyone join the rabbit in saying, "But please, oh please, don't chuck me into that briar patch!" Use a squeaky little voice, with a southern drawl, if you can. Have everyone scream and shout with the rabbit, as well, when he's in the briar patch.

The Crocodile Brother

Divide your crowd into three groups. Have one group play the crocodile, grinning, opening their mouths wide, and snapping their jaws shut with a growl. Have another group play the chicken, clucking when the chicken is mentioned, and saying, in a chicken voice, "My brother, please spare my life. Find something else for your supper." Have the last group play the duck, quacking when the duck is mentioned, and saying, in a duck voice, "My brother, please spare my life. Find something else for your supper."

The Boastful Toad

Divide your crowd into four groups. Have the first group boast, "I can jump much higher than you!" while jumping in the air. Have the second group boast, "I can kill more flies than you!" while sticking out their tongues like frogs and slurping up pretend flies. Have the third group boast, "I can swim much further than you!" while making frog-swimming motions. Have the fourth group boast, "I can make myself bigger than you!" while sucking in a big breath of air. And then have everyone suck in big breaths of air along with the boastful toad.

The Clever Mouse Deer

Have everyone make elephant, pig, and ape noises at the beginning of the story.

The Ant and the Grasshopper

Lead everyone in a big yawn and then, with a sleepy voice, have them say Grasshopper's line with you: "Come and sit with me for a while!" You'll need to do it in a shivery voice the final time. Have them say "Can't" with Ant in a sharp and squeaky little voice, as well.

You could divide the group into two instead, and have one group play Grasshopper and the other play Ant.

Big Jack, Little Jack and the Farmer

Have your group play Farmer Fred, whooping and hollering with him in the first part of the story, making vrooming car noises and splashing swimming noises in the second part, and weeping and wailing noises in the last part.

Three Days of the Dragon

Have everyone roar, "The Legends!" when the dragon does. And have them jump up and own like they are the children on the dragon's belly.

How the Turkey Got Its Spots

Divide your group into two. Have one group play the lion – creeping and leaping and roaring and coughing and sneezing with him. Have the other group play the turkey, scratching and flapping and gobble-gobbling.

The Tortoise and the Fox

Have everyone play the tortoise, pulling their tops or jumpers up under their noses when he disappears inside his shell, shuddering and shivering with him when Leopard tries to get inside, and then sneaking away when he reaches the river bed.

The Generous Rabbit
Have everyone shiver and sneeze and walk through the snow with Rabbit (hopping, hands like ears), Donkey (hee-hawing, hands like ears as well), Sheep (baa-ing), and Squirrel (hand waving like bushy tail from behind) motions and voices.

The Noble Rooster
Have everyone "Cock-a-doodle-do!" with the rooster.

Rabbit and the Crops
You might want to make three simple props for this one. Use three large pieces of paper or card. Fold the first paper in half. Draw potatoes on the bottom half, and potato leaves on the top. Fold the second paper in half as well. Draw oat stalks on the bottom half, and oats on the top. Fold the third piece into thirds! Draw corn stalks on the bottom and leaves on the top. And put ears of sweetcorn in the middle. Then use them to tell the story.

The Woman and the Bird
Choose a volunteer or two or three to dance like the bird. Teach them a silly little dance – or let them make up their own. And have them dance every time the bird does.

The Mole's Bridegroom
Lead your group in playing the sun (make circle with arms and shout, "Shine!"), the sky (wave hands in sky and shout, "Sky!"), the clouds (point in the air and say, "Puffy!"), the wind (wave hands back and forth and say, "Whooo!"), and the earth (stomp feet and say in deep voice, "Earth!").

The Kind-hearted Crocodile
Divide your crowd into five groups. Have one group shout, "Dingos are for dinner!" The second group, "Roos are for stews!" The third group, "Koalas are for kebabing!" The fourth group, "Goannas are for garnishing!" The last group, "Platypuses are for pickling!"

Why the Tortoise Has No Hair
Have everyone make a rumbly tummy sound with the tortoise. Have them make a dribbly drooly sound with the tortoise. Have them slurp up the porridge with the tortoise. And then lead them in a big sigh when the tortoise looks into his hat at the end.

Big Jack, Little Jack and the Bird
Big Jack and Little Jack speak in couplets in this story. So divide your group into two. Have the first group repeat what Big Jack says after you, in a deep Big Jack voice. And have the second group repeat what Little Jack says, in a squeaky Little Jack voice.

It might also be fun to have a volunteer play the bird and several others to play all the "bad" Jacks, and then to have them link up and race around the room.

How the Rabbit Lost Its Tail
Have everyone turn their arm into the rabbit's tail: dragging it in a long, wavy motion; sticking it straight up into the air; making it bounce up and down. And when the tail is bitten off – turning the hand into a fist.

You could also make this a counting story and have everyone count the sharks with you in groups of ten. Practice it ahead of time.

The Badger Teapot
Divide your crowd into three groups. Have the first group make the "Ting-a-ling. Clang-clang. Plonkety-plonk" sound with you. Have the second group shout, "Hot! Hot! Much too hot!" with the badger. Have the third group clap and cheer with the crowd.

The Kind of Hungry Lion
Have everyone growl along with the lion's tummy, getting louder as it does.

The Big, Soft, Fluffy Bed
Have everyone "squeeeek" with the door, cry ("Boo-hoo-hoo") with Danny, "miaow" with the cat, "woof" with the dog, "oink" with the pig, and "neigh" with the pony. And you could have them snore with Danny at the end as well, when he finally goes to sleep!

The Peanut Boy

There's a little chorus to the story that builds as the story goes on. Teach your group the sounds and actions to that chorus and lead them along the way:

"Henry in a peanut shell": they scrunch up their faces, or surround a fist with an open hand. "Henry in a chicken": make a chicken sound. "Henry in a sly old fox": yipping sound. "Henry in a hungry wolf": howl. "Henry in a great big fish": glub. And Henry's mum and Henry's dad just talking in the kitchen: make talking hands.

The Wonderful Bird

Have everyone make the "Kekeko. Kekeko" (the accent is on the first syllable, I think!) sound with you. And have them say her name with you when it appears.

The Cat, the Mice and the Cheese

Have everyone play the mice – squeaking and squabbling in little mice voices whenever the mice do.

The Goats and the Hyena

Divide your crowd into three groups. Teach the first group the line "They are my horns, sir." And have them make horns on their heads with their fingers. The second group, "It is my woolly coat, sir." And have them wrap their arms around themselves. The third group, "Because I am afraid that you will eat me, sir." And have them chomp their teeth. Do all the lines in a na-a-a-ing goat voice. Then lead them in those lines when the first two goats answer the hyena.

The Clever Crows

You might like to use this as a maths/counting story, depending on the age of your group. So you could ask them to give the answer to the "adding up the pebbles" question.

You could also use coloured marbles for the pebbles and actually make the water rise in a bottle by adding them according to the story.

The Monkeys and the Mangoes

Ask your group what their favourite food is. Then tell them your favourite food and explain that whenever you think of your favourite food, you rub your tummy and go "Mmm". Tell them to think of their favourite food and say "Mmm" together. Then lead them in that sound whenever it appears in the story.

A note from the author

Most of the stories in this book are retellings of traditional tales from around the world. They have been retold by many people over the years and I am just the next in a long line of storytellers. Each of us uses slightly different words and phrases, and so the stories evolve. You may wish to read other versions of some of these stories, so I would like to acknowledge some of the sources I have referred to, although most of these stories can be found in several collections. You will not find the stories listed under the titles used in this book, but they should be easy to identify in the books I mention.

"The Peanut Boy" and "The Big, Soft, Fluffy Bed" from *10 Small Tales*, Celia Barker Lottridge, Margaret K. McElderry Books, New York, 1994. "The Fox and the Crow", "The Tortoise and the Hare", "Big Jack, Little Jack and the Donkey", "Big Jack, Little Jack and the Farmer" and "The Dog and the Wolf" from *Aesop,* or from *The Fables of La Fontaine*, Richard Scarry, Doubleday and Company Inc., Garden City, New York, 1963. "The Goats and the Hyena" from *Arab Folktales*, ed. Inea Bushnaq, Pantheon Books, New York, 1986. "The Mole's Bridegroom" from *Asian-Pacific Folktales and Legends*, ed. Jeannette Faurot, Touchstone, New York, 1995. "Big Jack, Little Jack and the Bird" from *A Book of Cats and Creatures*. "City Mouse and Country Mouse", "The Boastful Toad", "The Ant and the Grasshopper" and "The Clever Crows" from *Folk Lore and Fable*, The Harvard Classics, ed. Charles W. Eliot, P. F. Collier and Son Company, New York, 1909. "Why the Cat Falls on Her Feet" and "Why Dogs Chase Cats and Cats Chase Mice" from *The Folktale Cat*, Frank de Caro, Barnes and Noble Books, New York, 1992. "The Tortoise and the Fox" from *Folktales from India*, A. K. Ramanujan, Pantheon Books, New York, 1991. "The Clever Mouse Deer" and "The Wonderful Bird" from *Indonesian Fairy Tales*, Adele deLeeuw, Frederick Muller Limited, London. "The Monkeys and the Mangoes" from *The Jataka Tales*. "How the Rabbit Lost Its Tail" and "The Noble Rooster" from *Little One-Inch and Other Japanese Children's Favorite Stories*, ed. Florence Sakade, Charles E. Tuttle Company, Rutland, Vermont, 1984. "The Generous Rabbit" from *The Rabbit and the Turnip*, tr. Richard Sadler, Doubleday and Company Inc., Garden City, New York, 1968. "How the Turkey Got Its Spots" and "The Woman and the Bird" from *Tales from the African Plains*, Anne Gatti, Pavilion Books, London, 1994. "Rabbit and the Briar Patch" and "Rabbit and the Crops" from *A Treasury of American Folklore*, ed. B. A. Botkin, Crown Publishers, New York, 1944. "The Cat, the Mice and the Cheese" from *A Treasury of Jewish Folklore*, ed. Nathan Ausubel, Crown Publishers, New York, 1975. "The Lion's Advice", "Why Tortoise Has No Hair" and "The Kind Parrot" from *West African Folk Tales*, Jack Berry, Northwestern University Press, Evanston, Illinois, 1991. "The Crocodile Brother" from *Zoo of the Gods*, Anthony S. Mercatante, Harper and Row, New York, 1974.